INSIDE
THE
HOUSE
INSIDE

INSIDE THE HOUSE INSIDE

ROSALIND
GOLDSMITH

RONSDALE PRESS

Inside The House Inside
Copyright © 2025 Rosalind Goldsmith

All rights reserved, including those for text and data mining, A.I. training, and similar technologies. No part of this publication may be reproduced, stored in a retrieval system, or transmitted, in any form or by any means, without prior written permission of the publisher, or, in Canada, in the case of photocopying or other reprographic copying, a licence from Access Copyright (the Canadian Copyright Licensing Agency).

RONSDALE PRESS
125A – 1030 Denman Street, Vancouver, B.C. Canada V6G 2M6
www.ronsdalepress.com

Book design: David Lester
Cover illustration and design: David Lester
Editor: Robyn So

Ronsdale Press wishes to thank the following for their support of its publishing program: the Canada Council for the Arts, the Government of Canada, the British Columbia Arts Council, and the Province of British Columbia through the British Columbia Book Publishing Tax Credit program.

 Canada Council   Conseil des arts
for the Arts   du Canada
Canada

Library and Archives Canada Cataloguing in Publication

Title: Inside the house inside / Rosalind Goldsmith.
Other titles: Inside the house inside (Compilation)
Names: Goldsmith, Rosalind (Literary author), author.
Identifiers: Canadiana (print) 20240519140 | Canadiana (ebook) 20240519167 | ISBN 9781553807261
    (softcover) | ISBN 9781553807278 (EPUB)
    Subjects: LCGFT: Short stories.
    Classification: LCC PS8613.O445 I57 2025 | DDC C813/.6 – dc23

At Ronsdale Press we are committed to protecting the environment. To this end we are working with Canopy and printers to phase out our use of paper produced from ancient forests. This book is one step towards that goal.

This book is a work of fiction. Any names used or references to people, places or situations are fictitious.

Printed in Canada

CONTENTS

Forsythia · 3
Worse · 9
Night Room · 13
Hummingbirds · 17
The Sandcastle · 19
The Lammergeier · 23
Getting by on York Street · 25
A Simple Request · 29
Allen in Wildwood Park · 33
Leaving You · 40
Leased · 42
In the Field · 46
Muriel's Café · 49
Preening · 52
Carry On, Carry On · 58
Beyond Poland · 62
Inside the House Inside · 71
Wall of Glass · 75
The Fret · 81
Mamboo · 84
Laugh Riot · 91
Trackless · 95
Updraft · 99
Panic Room · 100
The Weak · 103

Burn Hectic · 104
Yellowcake · 106
Black Water · 109
(She Speaks in a Quiet Voice) · 113
come back & no don't · 116
Renter · 120
You   Body · 124
That Old Life · 127
Bone by Bone · 131
Tats and Torments · 135
Pest · 141
Stillchild · 146
Icicles · 148
The One About · 153
Swing · 157

Acknowledgements · 161

About the Author · 163

INSIDE
THE
HOUSE
INSIDE

FORSYTHIA

They were on a dirt road travelling south. Rick was driving fast, and the RV kicked up whole atmospheres of dust behind them. Susie had no idea where they were going, but she supposed he knew. They had picked up everything they owned, dumped it in the RV and left the house behind. They never did own much, now even less, now almost nothing. Her clothes, his clothes, some cash, not a lot, enough for a few weeks. And the old RV, ancient now, his father's once.

Fact is, they left the house because they lost the house, ran behind on payments, chasing after the mortgage for months on end and then not making the payments, sometimes not even getting close, and some months nearly there, borrowing from hell's own loan sharks, and her father, and racking up substantial sums of debt on the credit cards, taking from one, paying off another, paying down the interest, using that card to pay off the mortgage until and up to the day when the game was up and Rick couldn't do it anymore, Rick's job at the store gone, Susie flunked out every night from two jobs, waitressing at Denny's and shifts at Dollarama, and he could see it was killing her, it was no good, they weren't making it, they weren't going to make it not in any fool's blind imagination, as Rick said, those were his words.

"Clear up ahead," he said, glancing over. She was staring out the window, no expression, none that he could decipher anyway. She'd turned off the radio several minutes ago, so he thought she might have something to say. He was right.

"Slow down. You're going too fast."

"Just trying to get there, that's all."

"Get where?"

"We'll know when we see it."

"See what?" she said.

"Trailer park, nice riverbank with trees, or a lakeside spot we can park at for a few days."

"And then what?"

"Then? We'll see."

"'We'll see' isn't going to get us anywhere."

"And where is the anywhere you're thinking of especially?" he said.

Susie fell silent. No answer, not even an attempt at an answer or any kind of scolding or rebuke. She was too flunked out, he thought, too tired to even care. They drove and drove on this dirt road, Susie clenching the map, checking it from time to time, but this road wasn't marked, or she couldn't find it if it was. It seemed to go on forever. Fields beside were dried up, some burnt out, nothing growing. Some tire marks in places. Thin bands of dust blew out across the stubble, settled and then billowed into clouds that swept over the dirt road, picking up more dust and blinding everything.

Then the road became just a path and ended. Just like that. At the end of it was an empty field, cropped low or never grown, just dry sticks. Rick slowed to a stop. They both got out, stretched and looked around. Now what? Now what? No trees or anything, just this field. And then Rick spotted some kind of a structure over to the right, some distance away. Hard to tell what it was.

"Look," was all he said, and they began to walk over there. Susie stopped, went back, got a bottle of water out of the RV, drank, offered it to Rick. Rick drank, and they both set off over the dried grass, the hard earth, the sun beating down, blazing murder on their heads, hard to see, even.

Rick was hopeful as they walked.

"Could be here," he said.

"What could be here?"

"Where we stay. Over there in that cabin or whatever it is. Likely no one there. We can rebuild. Homestead. Homesteaders. Like the old pioneers. Whaddya say, Suze? Up for it? Begin again?"

He looked across at her, but she had nothing to say, so he went on, hoping to boost her up, hoping to find that bright lit-up Suzie he met once who was so keen, so eager for life and for a life with him, and they had planned it all out correctly in the way that they were told they should, and none of it, none of it had worked.

"And we could grow tomatoes maybe, and catch stuff. And I can build or rebuild whatever needs to be rebuilt. I'm handy, I could do it. Flowers could work in the front of the cabin, flowers and a few bushes or what have you, Suze, you like the little yellow ones that come out in the spring, what are they called?"

"Daffodils?"

"No, early in the spring, like a bush."

"Forsythia?"

"That's it. Forsythia. And who's Sythia, I would wonder."

She smiled. They walked on. He took her hand. He thought his head might split with the heat axing down through it. She felt hers cracking like an eggshell. In the city before they left, there were foolish kids frying eggs on the tarmac. It took five minutes, but they were cooked right through, hard yolks and all. Then they fried bacon on the hoods of cars, simmered beans in hub caps. It was a foolish thing, impressed nobody, least of all her. Kids were always foolish, she thought, that's the problem with them, they don't even see the seriousness of it and it's them too who will have to live with the seriousness of it. Shit for brains. The neighbour's kids. She lost the track, wandered off to the right, he took her hand again, redirecting her back to the path — not that there was a path, really, but there was at least an end in sight.

They walked, and as they walked the structure they were headed for began to reveal itself to them, and it was up for no good, this structure, because it was not more than a heap of burnt-out logs with some of the blackened posts still standing, like it had been a home once but was not anymore now because someone had torched it, had despaired and torched it, or had despaired and drunk to all forgetting and maybe dropped a burning cigarette down the backside of a sofa and torched it and incinerated themselves and anyone else in the cabin too. Possibly a whole family had been charred to ashes here. And all that was left was a higgledy-piggledy pile of old burnt-out logs, and where the kitchen may once have been, some shards of china and glass, a big iron frying pan and a sink — a kitchen sink — (ha ha) the "everything but" being the "nothing but" here.

And for some unknowable reason, Rick, and Susie, still hand in hand, stepped inside this ruin, if there was an inside, which there wasn't really. They just stepped from dirt to dirt and from dried grass to dried grass. But they knew they were in it when they were there. Because they felt a heaviness take hold of them as they stood there, like the weary sigh of the earth, or like it was the absence of those dwellers who fled or were burnt to ashes from despair, or who maybe drank themselves to their own death. They could feel the blight of it in their own hearts, and they stood silent, like in prayer, but they weren't praying, and they weren't thinking anything.

Then Susie stooped and picked up a log she was standing beside. As she lifted it, the half of it crumbled to black ash. And she dropped the other piece of it, which sent up a cloud of ash when it landed, thud on the ground in front of them. There was nothing underneath that log, where it had lain was just more ash, and more dirt under that. It was easy enough to see that there was nothing there.

"Not much here," Rick said.

"No, it's all burnt out."

"Still, it's some place, some place to be."

Susie looked at him, a hard question in her eye, he knew it, but couldn't help saying anyway, "Maybe we owe it to them, to rebuild."

Susie went quiet again, just stood there, her head hanging, so he let it rest for a moment, then he said, "We could stay for a while."

Susie nodded. They stood there and looked around for shade. None though, that they could see.

WORSE

He jerks to life — shock of waking — was dreaming in symphonies — a weird eleven-piece orchestra of eight harps, two cellos and one theremin — an unearthly shimmering of arpeggios, and a severe counter-note that held the bass and sounded a long and singing hool of an alarm, fear brimming up from there, from the deep downing sound. When he awoke from that unremembered dream, he was in a flying panic — was sure he owned a dog, a slim thinning whippet of a dog that he'd forgotten to feed for weeks and weeks and now it was whining pathetically somewhere off to his right. But nonono. He had no dog — it must have entered his consciousness from somewhere in his room.

He believed the atoms of thoughts and dreams could be left behind in the physical world — in a particle of matter or in a molecule of moisture, a thumbprint or a sneeze, and he believed that when we pass by those slipped atoms, we might attract them somehow and then they would stick to us like transparent film, or insinuate themselves into us like a gas, or explode supernova-like within us — and he believed this is how the world becomes moreso — how we invent things and such, by collecting these restless atoms of thought and image. Then, we turn them over in our hands, piece them together into something we can use, patch this onto that, tack that onto this, reconfiguring stalagmites of matter into new designs and structures which exist no longer than seconds then dissolve back into the *Ewigkeit* and become once again: atom.

And so, he believed the dog, the whisp of a whippet of a dog, was somewhere in mid-air, chasing around up there — a memory belonging to his friend who had passed through his room yesterday, blinked or coughed and left the after-image behind him in a molecule of breathed moisture.

Nothing he could do with it now, he decided, so he let it chase its own tail in the mid-air of his room, leaving it up there to jazz and circle, and he was relieved he had no real dog he had forgotten to feed and no such responsibility and no such grief.

He was determined to start this day well — hell-bent and duty-bound for getting up today, for attacking moments like tennis balls coming at him, and swatting them back with a precise, focused intention. Yes, get up, get set into the day, move into that future panoramic afire with possibilities: a fine job, a fine friend, a fine flaming girlfriend, a fine place to live, a twittering hyperbole of conversation, the ranting and the revelling in the new economy — the sharing of it and the lovingness of it, the new caring of the new world, the new worthwhile birth of a new world for all — hell, yes. No poverty, no unkindness. This new waking world of love and harmony. Get up to it. Face into it. Step out for it. It's there.

It only waits for you to enter into it and book a room. All credit cards accepted, preferred customer take advantage of this offer while you can. Hell. Yes.

He did not get up. He looked out his window and saw the storming of the world, the flaring of the sun, the way the grass was burning up and the earth parching to dust. Sand was piling up on the outside sill of his window, light tarnishing glass.

A rust-like haze hung in the sky, a blur of light that seemed to bend, waver and crenellate right above him, as if the sky had taken on a freakish substance of its own and was now beginning to crumple in the storming and in the heat.

Or:

It could be, he thought, that some foolish someone, daring to walk outside in the sear of the day, was thinking of: corrugated steel and the picture of it hung in the sky, hung and was raised up in the sky and became memory of steel suspended in air.

Or:

It was, simple enough, his own crushed and shattered state of mind: a lingering of the dreams he had in the night, the tracings of tequila and vodka he drank with his friend, or the remnants of psilocybin dancing streaks and slashes of bended light in the air above, all mere hallucination, mere mirage, the false impressions of the fickle light. It was either some such antic thing, or it was something worse.

And:

The something worse was, he knew, only the real thing

that was happening in the world outside his own window and with it the undeniable voltage of alarm, the vertigo of no response, no possible response now, it being too late; and in the weird empty silence of the no reply, the thickening air folded in and folded in and became implicate matter.

And in his room, he closes his eyes to dream better, to dream kinder than the worse of this. Dreaming now in tones and memories of white lilac and white freesia falling under dove-grey skies, and the tuning of theremins and harps in wide woven harmonies and cool breezes coming in now from the east and from the north.

NIGHT ROOM

In the room, they talked — just the two of them — in total darkness, harrowing through the losses, the hurts, the threats. This small room — in the basement — thick black walls, cement floor — came with the house. They left it empty when they first moved in. But one night, standing in the unlit room, deciding how it could be used — maybe laundry, maybe storage — they began to speak — memories and dreams, creatures and images arose from within.

She told him her nightmare of a horse on fire. He told her of a cockroach he'd once found on his pillow that crawled into his sleep, night after night. They spoke for hours.

Over the days and weeks, they retreated to the room more and more often — whenever their fear overcame them and they couldn't tolerate what was above.

They could have talked to each other anywhere in the house. The bedroom was spacious and full of light, the kitchen warm and cozy with a round breakfast table — the perfect place to sit and chat over coffee. They never did. He fixed his gaze on the news, she scrolled through Facebook and Twitter. The few words exchanged in daylight were the dull currency of praxis, the normal and the dead.

When they went down to the Night Room, they would shut the door, sit on the plain wooden chairs they'd placed in the middle of the room and speak quietly to each other in the gentle siege of dark.

They spoke of shocks, of moments that had twisted their lives, affinities that were new and unfamiliar to them. She spoke of a wild yellow dog with black eyes, a terror that stalked her by day and by night. He told her of an ant he'd once burned with a magnifying glass — how the ant shrivelled in the tiny sun he'd created, the singed legs curling up, the thread of smoke. His horror at what he'd done.

They never spoke of the strangeness of the Night Room; they spun a world out of the dark. It became their home.

And if one of them was worried about the threat, they spoke of that too — as an old vengeful workman going round from house to house, smashing windows, or as a cloud of locusts. And they would speak to each other until their ragged feelings could be sewn up smooth, simply by listening. At times, they sat in purest silence and didn't speak at all.

After weeks and months, they spent so much time in the Night Room they no longer felt comfortable anywhere else in the house. They shuffled about in it and hardly spoke. Didn't look where they were going and sometimes bumped into each other on the stairs. They were strangers to the house and barely spoke to each other. She would pick up a cracked vase and put it back down on the mantle. He would stand and stare out the bedroom window and then draw the curtains.

They took to writing messages on the kitchen table with a Sharpie, the walls of the kitchen bristled with sticky notes. They stopped cleaning the house, stopped doing laundry. Rarely went out, except to do shopping.

The fridge broke down. They didn't get it fixed. A leak from a bathroom pipe soaked through the kitchen ceiling, spreading into a wide stain and dripping onto the kitchen floor. He placed a plastic bucket under the drip.

That night they retreated to the Night Room and had a long rambling talk about furies and sirens, dark seas, wooden ships. The earth shedding its skin in volcanic ash. The river of Xanthus. The time it took a giraffe to swallow. Blood skies.

Their dreams crept with the living creatures of their long, fathomless talks. Myrmidons marched, horses with manes of fire ran fearless across open fields and dry riverbeds, bright ribboning sunsets scattered a rum light on calm seas and bathed their fears in long-reaching shadows. So that they would awake refreshed and ready to descend again to the basement. They spent hours and hours in the Night Room, until eventually, most of their day and night was lived there. They brought down a mattress and a blanket and only went upstairs to use the washroom or eat.

Once when they went upstairs, they found some chicken bones, a blue raincoat and a trilby hat on the kitchen floor. He put a padlock on the door of the Night Room, a deadbolt and a chain lock so no beast, no phantom could enter.

They carried down packages of food. He drilled a small hole through the brick wall to the outside to let some air in close to the ceiling. From time to time they could hear creaking noises as the wooden stairs warped. Once they heard a ripping sound as if someone was shredding paper. And always the drip drip of water into the bucket in the kitchen above.

One night the living room window smashed and the wind flew in and howled through the empty house above them. He boarded the window the next morning but didn't have enough wood to cover it, so merely placed two planks in a big X across the empty space. He didn't clear up the shattered glass. From that time on, they heard the steps of animals, the clicking of their nails on the linoleum floor of the kitchen.

On a morning that they didn't know was morning, they ran out of food. They were sitting on the floor of the Night Room, their legs stretched out, their heads lolling. They dozed and exchanged single words or names, a wake of silence flowing behind each one.

After a long drowsing stillness that lasted days, they felt a weight pressing down from above as if the ceiling were sinking and the air in the room thickening. And then—a long slow groan of agony as if the floors and walls above them were bending and collapsing. For many hours they endured this pressure, this noise. Finally, he unhooked the chain lock, slid the deadbolt across and opened the door. He didn't say if he would return. She heard his cautious steps on the basement stairs. Then, quiet.

His slow steps returning. He came back into the room, locked the door, drew the deadbolt across and sat beside her, holding her close.

HUMMINGBIRDS

That year all the hummingbirds died, their tiny wings folded in on sorrow. They lay strewn across our wide yards like dropped commas, delicate in their death and some even said eloquent. But what was it they were trying to say to us? Maybe they wanted to inscribe a vision upon our minds, a vision we would never forget, and it was true, we never did forget their deaths, the picture of them fallen and silent.

Some people told us they even saw them fall from the sky, but we didn't believe them—it happened suddenly, catastrophically, intentionally, at night. We tried to find the meaning in it—all of us did—beautiful songs were written—poems and stories, but no one came close to finding the meaning of it, no matter how hard we tried.

Prizes were offered too—a set of cut-glass goblets, an antique golden watch, a real hair dryer. And the prizes encouraged us to try even harder. But the more we spoke of the death of the birds, the less we understood, and the more confused we became—though we preserved our sanity by celebrating the poets and the songwriters and storytellers who sometimes dazzled us with elaborate explanations.

Theo Murray next door decided he would bury all the ones he found in his backyard — and so he did, he dug 103 tiny holes in the dirt and buried them one by one, wrapping each one in a thin tissue, folding the leaves over and over and placing each tiny carcass in its grave, scraping the loose earth over and placing a pebble as a marker. He knelt by each grave, folded his hands on his lap and closed his eyes, tilting his head up to the ashen clouds, and his little lips murmured a soft prayer to each bird. His mother Diana, my good neighbour, could not bring him inside until he had buried every one.

Most people chose to gather the birds in old sailcloth or burlap and carry them out to the edge of the street. Special collectors were sent round with signs of wings on their chests to gather up the ones that had fallen on our yards and on public lands, and the weeping never stopped. All of us wept, we couldn't help it, there were public services held with prayers and chanting, and we found ways also to ease the sorrow — dancing, singing, drinking until drunk and toasting our prizewinners.

And all of us said how curious it was we never ever saw them when they were alive. We saw them only dead, and only dead they spoke to us.

THE SANDCASTLE

He didn't speak. He held out a handful of mints and offered them to her. She was sitting in the middle of the sandbox with an upside-down pail in front of her and sand islands on her knees and legs. He stood at the edge of the box and waited, holding out the wrapped green candies for her. He was standing there for a long time. Finally, she looked up.

"Are those for me?" she said and wiped her hands on the skirt of her orange dress.

But still he didn't say anything. She got up and stepped towards him. He stretched out his arm a little more to show her that the candies were meant for her. He didn't smile.

She took three and went back to her place in the middle of the sandbox, in front of the upside-down pail. "Come here," she said. "I am building a sandcastle. You can help me."

He stepped into the box and putting the rest of the candies in his pocket, sat down beside her. She filled the bucket with damp sand and turned it upside down. "There it is," she said, taking the bucket off. "A sandcastle. You can put something on top of it if you want."

The boy looked at it, picked up a handful of sand and drizzled it on top of the heap. Then with his other hand he flattened the thing.

"That's not nice," she said. "I made that."

He looked at her and stood up. Out of his pocket he took the remaining mints and dropped them into her lap. Then he walked away across the playground to the bench where his mother was waiting for him, book in hand. "Hello, Superman," she said.

He put his hand on her knee and lifted it up and down several times.

"What are you trying to say, Meeps?" she said.

But he just went on lifting his hand up and down on her leg and staring up at her.

"What is it? What's wrong? What happened?" she said, and she bent towards him to lift him up onto the bench. But he insisted on patting her leg over and over, and she thought it must be a new game he was playing, so she began to tap her other knee, copying him, because the therapist told her this can sometimes help, though sometimes not, but it doesn't hurt to try. But the boy pulled her hand away and kept hitting her knee with his hand, harder now, until it almost hurt.

"What's wrong, Meeps? Did someone hit you? Did that little girl hit you?"

He tilted his head, kept hitting her and hitting her, staring at her.

She bent forward, closer to him. "What do you want to tell me?"

He wanted to tell her this: the story of the little girl, the candies, the sandcastle, how he had destroyed it without knowing why it was not something he wanted to do. But he couldn't say it, couldn't tell it, couldn't even begin to search for the right words or any words to tell her his story.

And now, in his mind, the story evolved as elaborate and delicate pictures began to bloom: a stone castle, a field of emeralds by a dense forest of majestic trees that swept the rainbow sky with their long graceful fronds. And in the castle grounds, inside a moat of crystalline water, goats and sheep grazed and servants tended to them, carrying wooden buckets of water. And the little girl from the sandbox was there in the castle in a room of her own with rich tapestries of hunters and unicorns on the walls, and she sat in the middle of the room where there was a sandbox, and she was building a beautiful model of the castle she lived in, with turrets and long narrow windows and a castle keep, and she put six little orange flags atop each turret. And in his story now, he was sitting beside her and telling her how he loved her, how beautiful the castle she had built was and how he would like to live in it with her but could not — not now in any case — as his mother was getting worried. And he quickly memorized all the dimensions of the castle, of each room, of each turret, of each winding staircase. Then he thanked her for being kind to him and gifted her with handfuls of gems he had found in the forest and told her that one day they would meet again, and he would tell her all the secrets of his mind.

Now sounds began to scrape against each other in his head, causing him pain, and there was nothing he could do to keep track of them all, pull them apart or get them out. And in his frustration, he just kept hitting his mother's leg harder and harder. And then he began to moan.

His mother stood up and took him firmly by the hand. She knew the worst was on its way — she had to get him home. She held his hand tightly and they ran-walked-ran towards the car, where she would pause for a second to call her husband and tell him to get home now, straight away, please.

"It's alright, Meeps," she said as calmly as she could, "we're nearly there." But something like electricity was shooting through her chest as they got to the car, and her head was throbbing as she opened the door.

"It's ok," she said and lifted him in.

But it was not ok. It was never ok. As she settled him into the car seat, she thought of the long difficult years ahead for her son. How would he manage when she and her husband were gone? How would he manage in five years, in three, in one?

He could not communicate, understood so little, could not reason and had no emotional life, no imaginative life at all. How could he live on this earth? What kind of a life could he possibly have? She wept, making no noise.

She wiped the tears, smiled into his face and buckled him into the car seat, her fingers fumbling as she tried to close the clasp. Just then he began to howl.

THE LAMMERGEIER

Inside: he hides under the kitchen table, crouching himself small into rat or mole, hugging his knees tight, squeezing his eyes shut. His father stands — not two feet away — yelling and smashing the good china dinner plates against the wall. His mother: cowering in a corner crying, her head hidden under her sparrow arms.

The father's back is to him now, and the boy sneaks out, runs runs out of the kitchen, down the darkened hall, out the front door, round the house and across the backyard, past the swings, past the apple tree, climbs the split-rail fence and throws himself into the fallows of a barren field full of weeds, thistles, crabgrass, the hard dirt huffing up dust as he picks himself up and runs, arms cartwheeling, chest burning. He heads for the tree at the end of the field. He can hide himself there, wait til it blows over. It's a small tree, and bare, but known. His sacred place, his territory.

A bird though: He sees it just as it alights on a branch, folding its wings into its body — enormous, a monster, white and black, with rust-red feathers staining its neck and head —

a wing span of at least eight feet—a savage hook of a beak, long white tufted legs. It flicks its head from side to side, then curves under its wing and sleeps.

And that's when the boy guesses it's safe to approach. He walks through the field towards the bare tree and stands underneath, looks up in awe. He's mesmerized by the bird's size, its Captain Hook talons, and moves closer until he is right underneath the branch where the bird sleeps.

As he stands, looking up, the bird lifts its head and dips it down, peers with one eye at the boy. It opens its dread wings, unfolds them full wide and lifts its body off the branch.

All jello now, the boy tries to bolt. He's no match—and in less than a second the bird catches up to him, its wings casting a deep shadow over the boy as it veers and swoops down, grasps the boy by the shoulders and lifts him right up into the air.

The boy screams, the bird screeches, carries him to the top of a cliff where it attacks him, claw to neck, beak to eyes, the face in ribbons now. With bloodied baby arms, the boy tries to defend himself. No good. The bird tears at his flesh, hooks and rips and rips and tears til finally, the squalling creature is still. The bird presses its head and neck and chest into the blood of the boy til its feathers are stained bright red with it. And the bird sits triumphant over its prey, preening blood into its feathers. Proud.

Inside the house: The mother sweeps up the shattered china. The father turns on the television, stretches out on the sofa, combs his hair.

GETTING BY ON YORK STREET

Seanna slumps, exhausted. Her tent is rat-shredded, pocked with holes, covered with an old tarp. Inside, her bed is a plastic mattress covered with dumpster blankets and a damp pillow. Two bags of clothes beside. A Coleman stove crouches in one corner—a kettle on it she hasn't used in years.

She sits on the pavement outside her tent, squinting at the people as they walk by. Her old green pants torn up to the knee, denim shirt worn and faded white, shoes wrapped up in duct tape. A front tooth fell out yesterday, now the other one feels loose, could be out by tomorrow. One thieving loss after another.

Other tent dwellers are camped out beside her. "The damned derelicts of the damned old defeated world" she calls them. They are loud, they scream, convulse, cough up blood, pass out. Sometimes they are rescued, sometimes not. They leave her alone now—anything she ever had of value already filched years ago. She's old and doesn't ask for much. No one speaks to her. She speaks to no one.

At night she thinks: What is there now to sustain? And why on this earth should I be sustained? Everyone she once knew — her people, her family — gone — distant or dead. Sometimes she's got money for vodka, sometimes not. The head that wakes her every morning vice-gripped with pain, the bones fevered with the cold, her pulse fluttering like a hummingbird trying to escape.

This morning she pushes a clump of matted hair away from her face as she watches the parade of the Haves marching by in lockstep on their way to work. God. They are so determined to live their lives as if it's worth it. As if life has something to offer them, or they it. She feels sorry for them, never envies what they have. She knows what they have doesn't add up to anything. It's just they don't know it yet.

If she can cop a few coins, she'll eat. If not, she won't. Today, she's determined to match the enthusiasm of the paraders. She says "Good morning!" to each one. And smiles.

This smile — a masterpiece. This smile — a life's work. This smile costing her everything she ever was: it's a childhood memory of a swing and a party dress, a moment of laughter shared with a man she loved who died twenty years back. This smile dredged out from the earthed ruins of her happiness. She dredges it out because she has to. It's a question of survival, survival a question of habit, habit hard to shake.

A young man passes by — he catches that smile — it reminds him of his aunt he hasn't seen in years, but he's not aware of that — he just knows he must go back. He stops, retraces his steps, puts a five-dollar bill in her paper cup.

"You have a nice day," he says.

"Thank you, you too," she says and pockets the bill.

He walks on.

She'll eat tonight. An egg salad sandwich with a large cup of coffee, and cream and sugar in it.

She knows this, but doesn't give it much credit—the fact of eating, the fact of living on. She thinks about the homicidal circumstances of her life. It's like her life has been bullied down by the days, and willed forward beyond its end date, and she doesn't know why. Why does she—why does it—bother? What's left now to hold on to? Clear enough: nothing. But it's a stupid, blind-eyed brute, the will to survive—and hard to wrestle it down.

At four o'clock it starts to rain, a driving, soul-flattening rain. She crawls into her tent and sits on the mattress. That tarp is supposed to protect her, but it's no match. The rain soaks through and drenches her, soaks her blankets, her pillow, floods out the bottom of the tent. This is bad. As bad as it can get.

Seanna crawls out. No point in being in there anymore. The street is filling up fast and flooding.

Her neighbour—a meth addict who pitched in beside her months ago—is sitting folded up and hugging his knees, his hoodie and jeans soaked through. Like her, he's staring at the rain. He's dishevelled and beaten down, drowning, like her, a creature almost obliterated by the rain, shivering and suffering and enduring and cold to the bone and to the marrow of the bone.

Debris floats by—coat hangers, a baby's shoe, a plastic seat cover, a doll's legs, wooden blocks—she watches it all go by. Hasn't got the will to go anywhere to get out of the rain. She's a part of it now, a part of this downpouring—feels absorbed and taken up by it—feels comfort. The last, no-hope kind of comfort. A release, a capitulation. All resistance gone.

At the curb just in front of her something floats by, sticking up out of the water. She reaches out for it—it's a small green plastic vase. She grabs it. Turns it over in her hands. For a fleeting second it reminds her of—

A promise once given her, long ago, by the man she once loved. A promise he couldn't keep, and with it: a white lily. How she put that flower in a vase, and the vase on her white windowsill. How he kissed her then. The black and white tiles on the kitchen floor. Her red wooden table. His eyes.

Out of kindness to her, this memory dissolves in an instant and washes away with the rain. But she keeps the plastic vase, tucks it into her pocket and watches as the waters rise, as the wide, rivering street flows by.

The meth boy beside her curls up into a ball, like an armadillo, as if making himself small will protect him somehow, as if, in his way, he is still capable of resistance.

A SIMPLE REQUEST

I'm standing in the produce section, somewhere between the carrots and the rapini, and I see a guy standing by a load of boxes, holding a bunch of Swiss chard.

"Owner around?" I say.

"What for?"

"Just — want a word."

He ambles over to a cashier. I'm following close behind. I know how quickly these missions can fall apart, then you're right back in the produce section, asking someone else if you can speak to the owner. The cashier picks up the phone. "Vincenzo to aisle seven," I hear on the loudspeaker. I'm standing back now, and nod to the guy as he returns to his boxes of chard.

The cashier's phone rings. There's a pause and I hear her say, "Customer wants to speak to you."

This must be a rare enough request because I'm expecting to wait at least five minutes, but Vincenzo turns up in two. His face is bloaty, blotchy and slack like he just got out of the toilet after throwing up an all-night binge. He's bald and there's a dent in his forehead—hoof-shaped, like the devil kicked him. Vincenzo is not happy. His eyes darken when he sees me. He's suspecting the worst, whatever that could be. I smile to reassure him it's nothing that serious, and I tell him my small request.

"It's just the snowplows in your parking lot?" I say. "They don't need to go out at three in the morning, do they? Maybe six would be ok? Could they do that? For the community? You see, all these houses around your parking lot—"

"The community, the community." He's thinking about this. "Those snowplows are going out at three in the morning? I didn't know that. I'll talk to them."

"Thanks," I say. "I appreciate it."

He frowns. The floor swallows him up. All of him. There's nothing left but this frown, which is nine parts anxiety and nine parts frustration.

"You know," he says, "some days you don't give a shit about things, and then other days you don't give a fuck. Know what I mean? This store is a piece of shit. I don't know why I'm here. This store is killing me. Look at these shelves, which they are by far too small and they are killing me. The back of this store is also about twenty times too small, and it is killing me too. Three weeks ago I get home and I get Bell's palsy. Know what that is? I'm sitting at the kitchen table and my face—it just fell—it collapsed on me like it had its own gravity, right here." He taps under his chin. "I thought my face was gonna fall off my skull. Know what I mean? I thought I was gonna have a heart attack."

"That's awful," I say. "It's the stress. It's not worth it."

A SIMPLE REQUEST

"That's what it is every fuckin' day. Stress. This shining shit heap of a store. I've told the mother company, just tear it down! Build a bigger store, with bigger shelves for fuck's sake. And a storage space at the back that is bigger than a bird's nest to contain rat shit. Anyway. The community," he says and looks at the floor. "I'm sure the community would be happier with a bigger store. Because this shithole is killing me."

I'm worried he's already forgotten my request. "There's nothing wrong with the store," I say. "Really. It's a fine store. It's just the snowplows going out at three in the morning."

"No, it's the store," he says. "It's the fuckin' store. It's gotta go. Don't you see it? The floor space is a tiny nightmare. Look at this catastrophe of a floor space here. You see this floor space? It is a fuckin' over-waxed kitchen tile. You see it, don't you?"

No, I don't see it at all, but I can't say that. "Well, I'm sure everything will be fine," I tell him. "I hope you feel better."

He shrugs and walks away. I can hear him muttering, "Community. Community. What the fuck do they know about this store? If they only knew…"

I go around to the back of the store to pick up a few cans of tuna and some rice. On my way to the cashier I take the far aisle, hoping I won't run into Vincenzo. But there he is, at the front of that very aisle, tapping into his cell phone. He glances up and sees me. I nod and smile. He draws a blank, stares. Then recognizes me.

"Oh, it's you. Madame Community, Madame Snowplow," he says. "I'm right on it, see?" He waves his phone at me.

"I'm gonna get right on it right away. I got about a million and one other things to do, but I'm on it. I'm all over this one. No more snowplows at three in the morning. I'm gonna wring their fuckin' necks before they do that again."

I smile and nod, wave and duck into a lineup. Ten dollars and twenty-five cents later, I'm on my way out of two places: the store where I get my groceries, and Vincenzo's eternal Vale of Misery.

I don't have much hope about the snowplows.

ALLEN IN WILDWOOD PARK

He stands by the tree, by the spread of roots of the tree, and the silence flares round him as brindled light, and the bracken shadows dapple the air, the green underfoot, the black turn of road beside him, and the mud between. Cross-branches etch lines and angles in the air, and the silence blooms mist-like around him, light-riven. Morning. He breathes. He is content here — here by this tall tree in this dim illumined wood inside the high stone walls.

The clothes are ragged on him — pants loose, belt hitched in, the end of it hanging, boots scuffed and sidling down on the well-worn outsides, the shirt ever-fading, the jacket arm ripped up one side, the collar frayed and the buttons gone. A smell from the jacket stuns, keeps people at bay. But he's not aware of the brute stench now, or the raggedness and scruff of his appearance.

In the group home they cut his hair weeks ago. They chopped, hacked, sheared. The grey of it sticks up now in patches like rough-cut straw. But he can't see it, could care less even if he could. Allen sees only out and above, hears what he sees, sees what he hears, takes it all in:

This shade-streaming island, sanctuary of mystifying light and shadows that blow green and sing with the green earth, brimming with the downy feel of stillness and the dark warm mud beneath. He breathes in all the tones. The subtle and the screaming.

The houses inside this great bordering stone wall: stately, somber and of a magnanimous stature — big-hearted, noblesse-oblige houses that could welcome entire families into a single kitchen larder. The corner he stands on by the tree hugs the garden of one such house — a mansion in the pure Georgian style. It is a sky-loving, white-bricked monument of a hundred cathedral rooms and a roof all smooth-tiled in sleekest black.

He sees through the trees the generous curve of a circular drive that sashays up to the front of the house. Within the circle: a full acre of lush green turf, magnolia trees, a shameless profusion of lilac and roses and blush peonies, all the singing colours of the possible universe.

Tiny impatiens chatter along the edges of the curving drive that fronts the grand Scarlett O'Hara staircase. Oh, a house like this one he's never seen before. The tower-high wall of glass on the third floor catches the shafts of morning sun through the trees and sends a whistling flash of light back to the sun. The song of birds glints in the air.

How he got here, he can't remember — only that he walked for miles and miles through the sear of the city — at least twenty miles — from street to street. He dared not stop for hunger for fear his hunger would be refused.

Now he is lost, far away from the group home, and no desire to return to that house now, with its throttlehold stench of stale smoke and urine, his unwindowed prisoneiric room — the narrow bed caved in on a broken spine, and his one possession — a high-class silver stereo player with speakers, a CD player and all — stolen by his ranting cagey thief of a roommate who would never admit it. No. Never.

He will not return to that house now and the screaming of tenants in the thrive of rage, or collapsed in the dark stairwell, drugged and laughing like birds, half-drowned and black-stained with the slick of despair. No. His only chance a fleet and final exit.

The wall around this neighbourhood is a fifteen-foot stone wall, high and threatful with shards of glass atop it. No fool — even in the extremis of need — would dare climb it. But he found an iron gate with a simple lift latch, which he simply lifted, and he walked straight into this gated paradise.

Now he stands by the tree at the corner of the road in the restful shade and in the dapple dim light and in the silence as deep and kind as the remembered sea: He dunked his head in once, long ago. At the beach with his sister and his parents. He ran out into the shallows, head-butted into the waves of the sea, embraced them and went right under. In that plunge, he felt the whale silence of underwater depths and it was love to him, all peace and grave green quiet. In the fretful years after, this was the feeling he'd tried to recover and never could. Until now. Here it is the same as the sea: plainsong quiet, smooth and kind, stone-walled against the noise of the city. He stands in a pure dark halo of warmth, the hush of shade to breathe in, a sighing and loving and humming silence. The blessing of shelter.

The seed of an idea opens within. He'll live here. He will find a way to make this his home. To hell with his carp-fish sister and his potato-eye social worker. They'll never find him here. He'll live in this park with its sentinel trees, its grand houses, each one dignified with its own car or two parked in the sleekish driveway:

Cars sleep like cats. It's still early morning, and they're all here: the Porsches, the Lexuses, the Rollses and the BMWs. He knows them all, has made it his job to know them all, and all the best ones are here, napping like Persians, Russian Blues or Siamese on their seal-back driveways. Soon their owners will come out, the engines will purr to life, and they will creep out softly through the silence.

Leaves rustle. A branch above cracks. A squirrel bounds, a hiccup of life beside him. Stops. Bounds. Scrabbles up the tree and is lost in the leaves above. The shadowy canopy begins to brighten a little, and he smells the spongy aroma of the damp earth and fresh hints of mown grass, remembers the taste of gentle white-tipped shoots.

He'll have to eat soon. Hunger gnaws. But he won't leave here, won't risk losing his place. If someone locks that gate, he'll never get in again. So. He'll wait. In a little while he'll find a sympathetic house. He knows the one — passed it on his way up the hill — that yellowish house with its rust-red roof, blue shutters and blue door. It cowers sheepish halfway up the hill, apart from the other houses, maybe intimidated by the grandeur of the older, nobler mansions. He'll knock on the blue door and ask for help.

For breakfast: four eggs on toast or toast and cereal. Please.

But first. He'll need to find a courage he doesn't have to confront the inhabitant of that house. He's no beggar. But circumstances compel. That's what he'll say. And he will do it. He will. But not yet. He'll just—wait a moment in case there is an offer. An offer is best. And maybe one will come soon, when the good noble people in the houses wake up and come outside.

For now, the time here is well spent, dwelling under this threnody of green light that fugues with the sifting shadows. Morning swells into silence. The earth seethes with kindness and warmth.

Soon soon, if no one comes out, he will choose his moment and walk back down the hill to the humble shepherd house with its blue shutters and blue door. He'll knock and it will be like this:

An old gentleman of late years and slow gait will answer the door and welcome him into his house and into the kitchen where he will feed him eggs and toast and cereal and coffee, and quiz him many questions about his life and how he ended up without a home and living gaunt, hunger-hewn and hunger-hurt out on the streets. And with a mouth full to brimming with cereal and milk, he will offer up all his answers, wiping away a pearl of milk off the table and telling the kindly old man the story of his life, not omitting his plans for the future.

He'll tell him about his seizures, and about his medications—the ones he took, the ones he flushed—about his father on the farm, baling the straw and the hay, and how his father died in the barn one night from a massive failure of the heart, the doctors said.

And about his sister—his sister who banked his inheritance after their father died, banked it in a trust account he's never seen and deposited him away in the city, in the first group home she could find—a dark, maggoty place, a black hive that would mildew the heart. His furies began then, flights of temper that leapt up and whipped round in a blinding firestorm he couldn't control.

It was the furies got him thrown out of six group homes—to the botherance of his social worker—and he felt the sting of guilt each time. And now he's out of the seventh. But this time it's different. He wasn't thrown out this time, no, he's out of it now on his own free-wheeling will, and he'll never go back. Never.

And he will tell the old man about the long talks he used to have with his father about architecture—the modern and the post-modern, the Georgian and the Regency. It was all in the books his father gave him too. He knows about all of it.

And sitting in front of the open-hearth fireplace with the old gentleman who has welcomed him in, he will tell him about his plans, all of them architectural, all composed in his head, down to the last fine detail, and he will even draw the diagrams for him. They will become friends.

There will be, in that kind house, the warm embrace of friendship, card games in the evening, the smiling over cups of tea and the laughing crackle of the open hearth.

But for now, until he can work up the courage to knock

on that door, he'll wait by this tree in case an offer comes his way. An offer is best. As the morning lengthens into afternoon, the good people are sure to come out from their grand palatine homes, and in their surprise at seeing him standing there by the tree in the midst of their paradise, they will approach him and smile and quiz him a few questions: "Who are you?" and "How have you come to be here?" and "Are you hungry at all?"

And then they will offer him food and a home here in this good sanctuary. And he will tell them how he loves it here — the green shadows, the sad light and rolling swells of silence like the waves of the sea. And finally, he will say he likes his eggs poached, but scrambled is alright, and if they have Tabasco?

He waits for someone to see him. The people come out of their noble houses, drive their cars away, walk their tiny footing dogs. But they never look at him standing there, waiting ever patient ever thinner ever lighter, his belt tightened another notch. He stands by the tree, by the spread of roots of the tree, as the darkening gathers heavy around him and the shadows shriek out in panic in the sundowning sky.

LEAVING YOU

What if a scorpion is a silverfish with a sting?

What if the colour yellow grew a tail?

What if a hydrangea had a heart attack? Would it die — or just fall off its stem and then climb back up again?

What if hate is edible sewage?

What if myopia is the love of an insect for an elephant?

What if a jury is a cluster of broken seashells on the shore, and the bottom of the ocean the look on your face when I tell you I have to leave?

What if your face is a twisted elastic, and what if mine is the bloated corpse of a laughing hyena?

What if you tell me not to go?

And what if I say: It's a pulmonary condition.

And if you sit down, you might be a horse trader with a rambunctious two-year-old colt on your hands — with killer hooves — or you might be a ginseng leaf dive-bombing in mid-air.

And if I walk away, I could be the colour of moss or the colour of a nebula never seen.

And if this sky were *not* falling, it would be a caretaker cleaning a hallway. But it is falling, it is falling and I have to go: Now.

Your eyes prescribe; they punctuate:

I would like to eat a hamburger — something I haven't had in years — and that's exactly what this is — this call to go, with ketchup and mustard and the works.

What if I stayed, you say.

Then I would be a hydrangea with a heart attack and you would be magenta and a sparrow with corvine tendencies.

And I would be the colour of hate and the taste of sand and salt water in your mouth after you drown.

What if I could explain and make some sense of all of this? Then I would be the ten of diamonds, and a tightrope walker and a laughing hyena and the root of a tree and the square root of minus one and a hallucinogenic drug you could inhale to the depths of your delight.

But I'm not. And I can't.

The colour of this is melanoma.

LEASED

I got home this morning at dawn. My landlord was taking out my bedroom dresser. He and his son-in-law were carrying it down the street—they got as far as the house two doors down before I caught up with them.

"Hey!" I said. "That's my dresser you've got there!"

They didn't say a word—just went on down the street, carrying it on their shoulders. They were both wearing long black coats and top hats. They cast long shadows under the blood-red sun.

I followed them. "I need—at least—some things from it at least," I said.

They put the dresser down on the sidewalk and turned their backs on me. The son-in-law lit a cigarette.

I opened the top drawer and pulled out a yellow scarf that once belonged to my mother. From the middle drawer I took a Christmas stocking my sister once knitted for me, and from the bottom drawer I chose a photograph of the family sitting together round the dining room table—it was old and had spots on it but I took it anyway—it was the only photo I had of us together. That's all I could carry.

"Just so you know," I said and pointed at them, "just so you realize…"

But they lifted the dresser and walked on down the street with it on their shoulders.

I walked back to the house. Out the front door came the landlord's mother. She was wearing a black hat with a wide brim and a black silk coat—and she was carrying my small wooden rocking chair.

"That's mine," I said. She ignored me.

I watched her as she followed my landlord and his son-in-law down the street. Couldn't see a van or a truck anywhere. But they all just kept marching away like they knew exactly where they were going.

I was just about to open the front door of the house—and out came the landlord's daughter, six years old. Her face was yellowish-grey. Her eyes wide and staring under a layer of blue eyeshadow. Her mouth yawned. She was dressed in a fluffy white dress with a gardenia pinned in her wispy golden hair—and she was carrying a stack of my books!

"Wait a minute," I said. "Before you go, I should just point out—"

She walked away from the house without a glance at me or even a blink. Jesus. Here's what got me—how can a six-year-old child carry a stack of books three feet high! How could she have the strength?

This time I got in through the front door and climbed the three flights of stairs to my apartment. Didn't see a soul on the way up.

The door to my apartment was open. Walked straight into the kitchen. My table and chairs were gone. Opened the fridge door. Empty. They even took my food, the bastards. All the cupboards bare. My dishes — with the blue fish on them — gone. My vitamins my cutlery my kettle — taken.

I didn't go into the living room — there was a strange chemical smell coming from there. The hall rug was gone. Bedroom door closed. I opened it. Nothing. No bed, no desk, no chair, no clothes. Curtains — but not mine — closed. I was just turning to go. A man was standing in the hall by the bedroom door.

"I live here," he said.

"Is that right?" I said and pushed past him. "Did you sign a lease? Because my lease hasn't run out."

"I don't need a lease," he said. He was a short fat stubby guy, that new tenant, chewing on a toothpick and staring at me like I was an intruder.

"Well, good luck," I said. "I mean with the landlord."

"I am the landlord," he said.

"Sure, fine, whatever you want."

I walked out and down the stairs. Didn't see anyone. Not the first-floor tenant or the tenant in the basement. I could hear her music playing faintly though. I thought of knocking on her door to ask her if she still had her lease — and her furniture. But I knew she wouldn't tell me out of fear of the landlord.

So I just walked out the front door and stood on the sidewalk to see which way my books and furniture had gone. No sign of anyone or anything. The street was empty and silent.

The fear got me then — that fear: Nowhere to go. No one to appeal to. No one to tell me what I was supposed to do next — or how I was supposed to do it. And no chance of compensation or reprieve. I got drenched and shivery with the fear. Shook it off. And it came back.

I walked in the other direction away from the landlord, his son-in-law, his mother, his ashen-face daughter, away from all the precious objects I owned and once held dear, and walked towards the police station in our precinct in order to file a complaint — a complaint I knew would never be heard, would never be filed, would never be recorded, considered or even glanced at — not even for a moment.

I walked and walked. The only other person I saw was a mailman coming towards me as I reached the corner of our street.

"Is there anything for me?" I said. "Because I'm moving. I have to move, you see."

He looked at me for a second and walked on by.

"Just wait a minute," I said. "I want you to know that—"

He broke into a run and disappeared down my street.

I was getting tired. I plodded on step after step away from the house and towards the police station — trying to remember exactly where it was. Each step became heavier and heavier until I finally sat down on a bench by the road. Where I once lived was gone. The sun bled out white.

IN THE FIELD

Pain? No. Glorious absence, for once. She breathed. She looked. Around her, wild mustard, dandelions and blue cornflowers pocked the field with colour. All was sun-drenched and ablaze with the high light. They walked through it, she picked a few golden lupines, no need to speak.

Then the pain came up again, brazen, hectic. She bent forward, hands on knees. He held her as she gulped air, straightened herself. They walked on.

"Ok?" he said.

"Ok," she said.

"Should we go home?"

"No," she said.

Moments then, when there was no pain. And the light flared and bloomed around the edges of the poplar trees that bordered the field, and it was intense, the light, coaxing every flower and blade of grass into the full fathom depth of its own colour and into a harsh beauty. She felt she was walking through a world lashed in light and rich in meaning, every branch and every flower glassed by the sun. And still they did not speak. After all these years, no need.

At the edge of the field, just ahead of them and to the left, a dog edged forward under the low rail of a wooden fence. It watched them, hackles spiked, black lips curled.

"Keep walking," he said. "It'll go away."

But it didn't. It followed them, by the edge of the fence, wouldn't let them out of its scavenging sight.

It was a blood dog, a hunter. Manged and blade-thin. The face was all black, black to the eyes and the eyes yellow. It had the hackles still up and the gall to shamble up to them, edging along beside them as they walked. It growled low and deep, the sound of a threat in its gullet.

"Don't look at it," he said.

They walked on. The dog kept a cringing pace with them, lying low to the ground and creeping forward through the grass.

"Throw something at it," she whispered. "Can't you?"

"No, that's the worst thing to do."

The dog growled as it crept along beside them, its back roached, tail tucked under, the fur all round its neck thick with the fear and the threat, as if a dementing wind raised it. From time to time it would stop. Just stop. Until they thought it was gone. Then it would catch up to them again, showing its teeth, rotten-to-the-root yellowed teeth.

They got to the far end of the field. The car was just down the road. Slowly, he opened a gate and helped her through. Closed it. The dog didn't follow. It sat by the gate and watched them as they left, yellow-eyed sentinel. Just before they reached the car, she turned back to look. The dog was slinking away from them, slowly weaving its way back through tall grass and wildflowers.

The light was all changed now, dulled to a grey cast, a withering stare of light that shrouded the field in a pale, glaucous bloom.

MURIEL'S CAFÉ

It was 2:00 in the morning. I broke into Sonya's house through the side door and climbed a few steps to the kitchen. I knew the room well. Crept over to the far wall and sat on the floor hugging my knees. It was cold. Dark. I waited.

Sonya's daughter Ashley was sitting beside me next to the stove. From its little green clock light, I could see she was half-asleep and not surprised to see me. She yawned and rested her head against the side of the oven.

After a few minutes, I heard a creak on the back stairs. The light came on. More creaks as someone came down the stairs. Sonya. She was wrapped in a thin white robe. Her hair was sticking out, her face papery in the harsh hall light. She stopped on the third step from the bottom, holding the rail. Looked at me.

"You," she said.

"Yes."

"It's not over yet," she said.

"Of course not," I said. "I'm sure everything will be fine."

Ashley rubbed her face and peeked round the stove up at Sonya.

"Go back to bed, Mum," Ashley said. "It's too late."

Sonya stood on the third step, looking at us. Ashley curled up against the wall and closed her eyes.

Sonya turned and climbed back up the stairs. The light went out.

I left the house twenty minutes later.

It was about 3:30 now. I walked down dark empty streets. There was a thin flashing glow a few blocks away, and I made my way towards it. It was a sign: Muriel's Café. Open. I crept in and sat at a table by the door. No cutlery. No menu.

Someone was sitting at a table on the other side of the door. I couldn't see them because it was darker on that side of the café. I blinked and adjusted my eyes to the dim light across from me.

Sonya.

"In the tropics there's a tincture that comes from a spider's venom," she said. She pushed the hair back from her eyes and told me how it could cure all kinds of ills, from internal hemorrhaging to warts.

"Will it work?" I said.

"Yes, I think so," she said.

A waitress shuffled into the room from the back. I could see the kitchen light as the door swung to and fro. She was wearing a white apron and a little white hat with a red border.

"What'll you have?" she said to me. Her lipstick was smeared all over the right side of her face.

I shook my head. She walked over to Sonya. I heard them

speaking but couldn't make out what they were saying.

The waitress turned back towards me and stopped at my table. She looked down at me — like she was going to cry or scream. "I can't help her," she said and shuffled back towards the kitchen.

The door swung to and fro. The yellow light from the kitchen came and went.

PREENING

He was standing in front of the bathroom mirror—knowing it was futile—most of his hair gone now, only three or four strands in the front hanging down from his skull, and six or seven from the back—he'd counted them—but still he preened. He put baby oil on the strands in the front and coaxed them over the top of his head. A scant—pathetic—little combover. But good Lord! What else could he do?

What was left to him now but to survey, to calculate, to take the measure of his changing appearance, in this—this last mirror left to him—to study his reflection just to make sure there was something of him left in that reflection—nothing much that was recognizable to him, true—but he was still there. There was his face, haggard and sagging, and his sluggish eyes, staring back at him—fish eyes or hollow Easter eggs painted to look like eyes—there they were, those things, staring back at him.

But all things considered—and if he squinted—he thought he looked alright—passable at least—though he didn't dare open his mouth—that was not a good idea—God knows what was going on in there, he didn't want to see. It frightened him awfully and he ought to call someone, someone to come and visit him—not to, not to—take *care* of him—good Lord, no! This was bad enough on his own. He wouldn't land this on anyone. But someone to sit with him for a few minutes to keep him company, someone who would speak to him—given his strange and disturbing appearance, and given he only had seven hairs left on his head, or possibly twelve. Who would want to speak to him now? Well, who?

He stared at his nose in the mirror. It looked like greyish wax slipping down a candle—so his nose was changing also—he was dissolving—who could he call?

In his mind that was no longer really a mind but more like a thick wad of damp, tangled moss stuffed into his skull, he went through a list of his friends in search of one who might sit with him—if only for a few minutes—he went through six—fewer than the hairs on his head—and ended up with one old friend he knew would oblige—if she had the time.

He made himself a cup of chamomile tea and called her. She sounded fragile, distant and a little surprised to hear from him after all this time, but—good Lord!—when he explained, she said she'd be over right away. She was a good one.

Twenty minutes later she arrived, surveyed his shabby and squalid little apartment and gave him a small paper bag.

They sat down on the worn old sofa in the living room which was also a kitchen, which was also a bedroom. She didn't seem to notice his changed appearance. At least, she said nothing about it. He offered her a drink but she refused.

She smiled. "It's good to see you after so long."

"And you," he said. His voice was hoarse from not speaking. "Thanks for coming over." He cleared his throat.

She smiled again.

"You haven't changed a bit," he said. "It's uncanny. You look just the same! You look great! So fine of you to come—so kind of you, after all this time."

"You look—" she began.

"You don't need to say," he cut in. "I only have seven hairs left on my head. Or twelve."

"Oh," she said.

It felt good to tell her the truth. It was a tremendous relief, really, to share this knowledge, this certainty of his change in appearance, and to see that she accepted it. He hoped, though, that she couldn't see the baby oil on his head—or see inside his mouth when he spoke.

His voice was still hoarse. "I meant to visit you that time, that time when you were—you know—I just couldn't," he said. "I couldn't handle it."

"It's ok," she said. "It's really ok. I understand. It's good to see you. All this time, you've been—"

"Away from you," he said.

"Yes," she said.

"It's been so difficult, these years, you know, not to have you here."

"I know," she said.

"We had—"

"I know."

"It was so damn *interesting* when I was with you, that's the thing." He pounded his fist on his knee. "I remember it all. I'm sorry I didn't—"

"No need," she said and smiled. "'Sorry' doesn't cut any ice now."

"Cut any ice…" he said. "I'm not sure I know what that means…"

She shrugged. "Since the water underneath is always dark."

Don't go cryptic on me, he thought, but didn't say it.

"And the ones who sink beneath the surface, when they go deep enough, they start to glow."

"Really?" he said. He was not going to challenge her in any way—didn't know what the hell she was talking about, but wanted her to stay.

"Please," he said. "Can't I offer you a drink? Vodka? Vodka and soda or orange juice or vodka and cranberry juice—your favourite—no, no I don't have any of that, but I have—"

"No thanks."

She smiled and crossed her legs. She was wearing that sweater she always used to wear so many years ago—brown and white—that comfortable, warm sweater with the curved, arcing pattern around the neck. Her favourite sweater. And his. It was who she was.

Her eyes were bright—kind of lit up, he thought.

"You ought to get that seen to," she said.

"What?"

"The inside of your mouth."

So, she had seen. He was devastated. Now he was sure she'd seen the baby oil glistening on his head.

"No, it doesn't matter," he said. "And by the way, I use baby oil only because it's—it's relaxing. It's not vanity, you know."

"God forbid it should be that!" She laughed. But he looked serious. "I didn't notice it," she said. "Really. I didn't." She smiled again in that way she used to smile when they walked through the neighbourhoods together and traded jokes, and traded ideas and said nasty things about the people they knew, loved each other to near insanity and felt loved, each one by the other.

She leaned forward. "And farther down beneath, I've seen creatures you couldn't even begin to imagine," she said.

"Is that right?" he said. "What kind of creatures?" He would keep asking her questions, to keep her there.

"Long flat beings with eyes on the top of their heads. Eyes that glow yellow and gold out of the depths. Some of them quite beautiful."

"I'm glad to hear it," he said. "Really glad." He wanted her to stay, not leave. Not now. Not ever.

"And strange plants that grow tall and sway back and forth in the currents, stretching out their arms, almost like they are dancing a minuet. They are also beautiful, and so many different colours."

"I'd like to see those," he said. "I really would. Maybe we could—"

Again, she smiled—this time that smile that seemed to be hiding something but probably meant nothing—because she always wanted to be a mystery to him. An unsolvable mystery.

She didn't stay long. After ten minutes, she got up and hugged him close. At the door she said, "It's not so bad, you know. You'll see. It's not what they tell you." He tried to hold her there, but she slipped out of his arms and left.

He went back to the couch. On the little table in front of it was the brown paper bag she'd been carrying. He opened it and looked in. He took out an oddly shaped little thing with branches. It rested in his hand. A piece of coral. *From God knows where she got that*, he thought, and put it back down on the table.

After a minute, he got up again. Slower. The pain slowed him and he shuffled into the bathroom and stood in front of the mirror. He opened his mouth wide. Then he moved one hair that had fallen to the side and placed it carefully back on the top of his head, and took out the bottle of baby oil.

"It's not so bad," he said.

CARRY ON, CARRY ON

It's a frenetic, willful, captious thing, this world, he said, and it may seem completely arbitrary, but it's not.

She was physically ok right now, maybe in remission, maybe not, maybe healing, maybe not, who knew — her heart wasn't in any kind of recovery, her mind gone off to some weird place. So she sought help, as people do, she thought, as people often do, it was no bad thing, it was help she needed.

The therapist's office was warm and welcoming, all done up in stark simplicity with low couches and low balsa wood tables and prints of bonsai and cherry trees on the pale green walls.

It's not arbitrary? Sandra said.

Do you believe it is? he said. Do you think it's out of your control?

The session lasted forty-five minutes and she left, dissatisfied as usual, knowing that none of this was helping. She'd been going to these sessions for six months now. Six months. When life is shorter, six months is longer. But she kept going out of habit and out of a sense of duty, feeling that if she didn't go, her therapist would be disappointed.

But the truth was there was no chance that anything he said was going to change any damn thing. Her mind was gone to a bad elsewhere and that was that.

No chance—like those group sessions when she was first diagnosed—Divine Power of Life. Each session was a makeshift refugee camp for the damned, where everyone shared the very worst, where no one could help anyone, where people cried like sick babies.

The only thing they shared was the misery of the condemned. And really out of the sixteen or so—sixteen to fourteen to ten to seven, the numbers dropped every week—*of course they did*—everyone hated—just hated—everyone else because this was a blackballed short-stick club of the damned that no one signed up for. And yet, here they all were, comparing their suffering like swatches of blood-stained fabric. Smiling and hating and smiling and hating. And desperate enough to hope that just attending these sessions could make death go away.

And every person in that hell knew like she knew—but wouldn't admit it—that none of this was going to make any difference. They were all going to die—most of them sooner than most, and nothing was going to save them from that—from the insanity of that insane fact.

It was the unacceptable truth and they were all trying to make it acceptable by "reframing" it, by turning it round and round in their hands until it became something more user-friendly—like, instead of a vicious agonizing death, My Little Pony or a strawberry ice cream cone. See: This is really not so bad. It's a good thing when you look at it the right way. It's all perception, all how you frame it in your mind.

Don't blame my mind! Sandra wanted to say to the facilitator.

That facilitator—she glowed with sympathy and sweetness—she fully embraced anything anyone said, standing there like she was some divine alchemist, trying to transform every miserable comment into something pleasant and palatable, something that fit well into her scheme of things that was just this:

A vague deathless existence in a vague deathless Disney World, with a Tinker Bell of love and compassion flitting around everywhere, touching everyone with the magic wand of transcendence—sparkle sparkle—which in her grand scheme meant climbing out of some kind of a swamp—that's what she called it—as if they were all alligators or lizards—into the clean air of the *Present Moment.*

Which was easy enough for her to say, standing there, since she wasn't dying and had *way* more present moments given to her than to anyone else in that room. And clearly, clearly, she didn't even believe any of it anyway. It was a pure lie. Sitting in that circle of hell, Sandra rejected all of it. It was all bullshit.

And when one of the members, who had a neck brace on and probably had no more than a month to live—when *she* started talking about picking up stones on a beach and seeing them as divine offerings to help us understand the endurance of nature etc. etc., Sandra could see that she was reframing those dirty old stones like crazy—turning them into messages from God; and then when the skeleton beside her spoke about her mother-in-law as a divine angel who was only sometimes a little thoughtless or unkind—Sandra could see it all clearly—that mother-in-law was probably a vicious old cow, and this poor sick woman was killing herself to reframe her as a fairy godmother—and that's when Sandra's mind left and went to that other weird place. That bad elsewhere. And that's when she stood up and left the room.

She walked right out of that Divine Power of Life and never went back.

Things went down from there. Her mind went darker and farther away every day, and so she started these sessions with this new therapist, who had it all worked out in his stark simplicity. The world was a harsh and indifferent place, he said to her, but within the harshness and inside the random throw of event, there was still a possibility of choice and a clear path to redemption. If we carry on.

Really? This was also bullshit.

After this last session with the therapist, she walked out and went to the park and sat under a tree. And under that tree there was a dead opossum. How the hell did that get there all the way from Texas or Alabama or wherever those things live? Elvis Presley used to eat those things fried, didn't he? There it lay, bloated and dead. Its eyes were bloated and dead and glassy, its mouth hawked open, a broken jaw. And the flies were swarming in around its jaw, and it was beginning to stink. And that was it. That was all. She didn't move from there.

Finally, finally.

BEYOND POLAND

Her body can't escape the cold, but her mind can. It casts up through the night, scattering itself into the sky over the Atlantic Ocean. It leaves her here—on this bench in the park—shivering, hugging her coat tight round her chest.

She came here when the last of herself ran out: laid off, out of cash—and now—evicted. In all her life, she never imagined this could happen—no warning, no hearing, no chance to explain.

The landlord thumped on the door til it rattled, then shoved his way in with two policemen. Told her she was trespassing—in her own home—she'd lived in this apartment for twelve years.

"I'm not leaving," she said.

They gave her enough time to pack a knapsack. Then the two officers grabbed her and held her arms above the elbow. Gripped so tight. Dragged her down and out onto the street. The street that was dark and led nowhere.

They threw her clothes out the window. She stood by and

watched as they fell like empty bodies from the third floor to the ground, no resistance. No substance. Limp.

She watched until the last of them — a red shirt she used to like — twisted and fluttered its way down to the sidewalk and lay there, dead. She picked it up. Dropped it. Walked away.

Alone.

Nothing. Only her knapsack and eighteen dollars cash in her pocket. She was hungry, found a variety store. Walked the aisles. Inspected and chose: three bags of sour cream and onion potato chips, four Mars bars — calculated — put one back. Three Mars bars and three cans of Coke.

She carried the items to the counter and laid them out in a neat line. Order here at least, in the shape and pattern of these things. "Is that all?" the cashier said.

It was bright in the store.

This man. He looked like a good man. Kind eyes.

The man said again: "Is that all?"

And she said: "Yes, that's all. Thanks."

It was a good, deep feeling to have this little exchange. Just like that. Meant nothing — this man didn't care — didn't know a thing about her or what just happened to her. The man uttered a few words, a simple question. But —

The words stayed with her, settled soft in her mind.

He had a warm, deep voice that seemed to come out of some distant place — to comfort her, to let her know that yes, there were good people out here, and yes, they did speak in a decent and good way.

Not all people were out to take away her job. Not all wanted to abandon her, evict her — throw her out onto the street. The dark street that led nowhere.

Those few words — they shone — beads of glass in a desert, scoured brilliant by the wind that blew the sand away — the wind that washed the words and left the words shining in the sun.

And yes!

She was young! Forty-three wasn't old. She could go on. This wasn't the end, was it? Couldn't possibly be.

She could take action: look for a new job. Find a place to live. Of course — but not a horrible shelter — a nice apartment, maybe smaller, yes, but that would be ok. Would be fine. Even just a room. She didn't need much. Didn't need anything.

She paid for the chips and the Mars bars and the Cokes and took her change: eighty-nine cents, put it in her pocket. Tied the shopping bag to her knapsack. Before she left, she said, "Thank you," and smiled as a gesture of hope and goodwill toward the cashier man behind the counter.

Silently, she wished him a good life, cradled and held fast by kind people who loved him. She wished him a life with a solid home, a level foundation and windows that brought in true light.

The man behind the counter didn't look at her again. But the kindness in his brown eyes was glorious and warm, insistent — like a memory of summer.

The door swung closed behind her. A soft little bell rang. And now: the street. The street that was dark and led nowhere. But: wait.

Human beings had long been nomads, and that's what she

was now: Linny, the Wanderer. A survivor in these cold, dark streets. Ok, this was — new — a tough break — but she could adapt. Adjust. Get strong. Begin again. Of course.

She was, after all, a creature of ingenuity. Resilient. Resourceful. She — as this creature — could find a way to go on. She'd scrabble in the dust if she had to, scavenge in the dead fields, unearth black roots and husks of seeds. Hunt rabbits, moles, even pigeons. Pursue. Kill. Live.

She'd start by finding a place to rest tonight. Sleep and dream hopeful. And tomorrow, the world would look different. Shock had cauterized her vision, that was all. In the morning, she would see clear and new and apply herself to the situation. First: look for a job.

And so, as darkness settled in, Linny found this bench in the park. She sat on its green metal back, ate a few potato chips and drank a can of Coke. The sweetness on her tongue. Oh.

She retied the bag to her knapsack and put them both underneath the bench.

She swept the bench with her hand to clean it, wrapped her coat around her body against the cold. Lay down on her side, bent her knees fetal. The bench was hard. Hurt her bones — her hip and her shoulder.

Closed her eyes. But sleep was nowhere. Sleep was back in her apartment, in her home that was taken away from her. She'd left sleep there, curled up cozy on her soft bed.

Now she was as cold as a fish on a stone. Knife poised above her gut. Cold as death. Gasping air. Glass eye of a dying fish.

She thought of the landlord and the two policemen who threw her out that afternoon. Felt again the shock of it in her stomach: swift plunge, hollowing out — the dread of losing her place under the sun. The dark street calling to her but leading nowhere.

And the cops had said: "You're being evicted" in their cold, hard voices — evicted — and the word measured her failure and redefined her in an instant as an unwanted thing — as useless, as unbelonged.

Severed. *Evicted*.

She threw up when they grabbed her. Her stomach betrayed her as it always did when she was anxious. Vomit down her coat. Humiliated. They took her down to the street — held her by her arms — above the elbow — gripped hard, dragged her out of her own apartment — a criminal. For God's sake. She'd done nothing wrong. For God's — a scruffy old neighbour was watching out her window, peeking out from behind her curtains. In her witnessing face, the glee.

People on the street watched as her clothes — her own clothes — tumbled out the window and twirled like shot birds down to the street. Her red shirt lying there — the one she used to wear when she went dancing at the Copa. What did her neighbours think of her? That old woman — everyone knew now. She was evicted — *an evict* — like a convict. Or a derelict — she belonged nowhere.

Only the street. The dark street.

She tried to wipe the vomit off her coat. But it stained yellow. Stamp of disapproval. Stamp of the reject. Mark of disdain.

On the bench, reliving all this, she turned herself over so as to put the pressure on the other side of her body. Her back ached and her right hip hurt. Her hair felt dirty, greasy. She pulled her coat up to her chin, the smell of it made her feel sick, but she dozed off for a few moments and saw—a vision—the shifting, variegated silhouette of a crowd moving into a massive stadium for a concert.

An opening and then a bright flood of light.

The people—their shadows—were opening their arms wide for her. The shadows held her close and she felt herself rising.

They lifted her high and she surfed the crowd, laughing, floating forward on thousands of hands. They carried her to the front of the arena, cheering. Then they laid her down on a flat stone. She opened her mouth to plead with them to lift her up again.

But the crowd dissolved into a dark blur.

She opened her eyes, conscious of where she was—on this hard bench in the park at 2:00 in the morning. And it was cold so cold, and her back and neck hurt her. She was hungry. She looked down under the bench. No oh no. Her knapsack her bag the chips and chocolate bars and Cokes—gone.

She sat up. Stood. Peered round in the grubby lamplight. Pulled her coat round her and began to run—first one way, then another—shadows of trees chased her—she had to find her knapsack and her bag of chips and chocolate bars and Cokes.

The thieves—it must have been a few minutes ago—she only just dozed off—why didn't she hear them?

She ran, rushed all around the park through patches of darkness, pools of light, back and forth down the street. Saw no one. Nothing.

Day broke cold.

She was limp with fatigue and sat down on the sidewalk outside a grocery store. A man walked by. "Do you have any change?" she said to him as he passed.

Linny had never said these words before in her life. They came out of her mouth like cockroaches she'd swallowed in the night.

The man didn't even look at her.

The stink of shame was all that was left of her now, the stain on her coat.

She gagged, she cried. Her mind shivered, dissolved into droplets and scattered over the sidewalk in front of her. Tiny globes of quicksilver were spilling onto the tarmac of the street. The dark street that led nowhere.

Her body sobbed and shook. It rattled the loose change in her pocket. Rattled the loose thoughts in her head. Cut free and drifting away.

She knew she could never say those words again. And if not? Then what. What would it be like to starve? She'd lived her life belly-full til this day. But even now an alien bitterness scraped at her guts. From the marrow out cold.

And tomorrow?

She started to yell as people walked by her on their way to work. She bellowed out from the pit of her hunger and from a slaughterhouse of fury.

If anyone heard her, they didn't show it. They walked

by. She had no money and no place to live. She didn't exist anymore. Yelling, she made no sound. She was a stain on the sidewalk. A mark on the cement.

A security guard was standing in front of her. "You can't stay here," the guard said. "You're trespassing." He picked her up off the sidewalk and held her arm above the elbow.

She tried to shake herself free, but the guard gripped her arm hard—as if she was a criminal. As if she never had a mother and a father, never wrote a story when she was six about a bear on water skis, never got an 88% on a math test in grade 10. She was society's garbage. An evict. Nothing more.

The guard dragged her down the street. Loosened his grip as they came to the corner. "Don't let me see you again," he said.

She walked away, fast, trying to think. Looked in shop windows for Help Wanted signs. Nothing. Picked up a discarded half-apple. Rotten. A crust of bread with a thin line of mayonnaise along the edge. She ate that. Sat down at a picnic table and rested her head on her arms. What could she buy with eighteen cents? She walked again and walked the hollow darkness in.

And here she is now, back on the same bench in the park, this iron bed. This unforgiving cold. Lying here in the night. Shivering. Knees curled up. Dozing in and out.

And it is now—this second night—that her mind lifts up. It casts wide over the Baltic Sea and beyond Poland. She feels the cold like rivers of ice flowing over her—but she breaks off from the pain and flies with her mind to wherever it might go.

It sails free and skyward far away to an Ultima Thule,

where fields of ice and blown snow wait for her.

The cold now is colder than any she's known—even worse than last night. Her skin shivers, her bones shake and her lips turn blue—but the sweetness is, here in this place, in these fields of snow, she can't feel the shame anymore, nor the fear. And now she can no longer even feel the cold.

Through drifts of snow, she sees a man approaching her. He's walking on snowshoes, using poles to pull himself forward. His head is down against the wind and he's moving slowly through swirls of white. Appearing then disappearing. Treading the flat round nets of his shoes on the sweeping drifts of snow.

The man comes up close. He stands above her and looks down at her. He's wearing a heavy coat with a fur-lined hood, and icicles hang from his eyebrows. His breath puffs up—clouds of white against the dazzle of white snow.

The ice man leans down low over her, and says: "Is that all?"

Oh! She feels the warmth of that voice and knows it instantly! And she sees the kind brown eyes too. The man is here to rescue her! "Thank you," she says. "I'll go with you." But the man turns his back, lifts his poles and walks away from her, disappearing into the blind drifts of snow.

She feels cold again, sheets of ice on her flesh.

Now, a lamp glows in the distance. In its dim light, Linny can see her red shirt flying up into the sky, winging its way down the street, carried off by the wind. She watches until it disappears, until the thieving night snatches it away, until all that's left is the long, dark street, calling to her.

INSIDE THE HOUSE INSIDE

She sits safe on a grassy bank by the stream eating handfuls of stale raisins, watches the water flow by. Little ripples and currents carry twigs and leaves downstream. She hears the croak of a frog from the other side — might try and catch it, might not.

This is a place to be away from the house — the grind and spit of what goes on in there. It's a small wooden house — on the outskirts of town — looks normal enough — but what goes on inside that house skewed way off normal long ago. And though she doesn't have much to compare her days with, she knows her days don't go right — no no — what goes on in that house is not what goes on in other houses, surely?

Curtains drawn, bedroom light off until 2:00 in the afternoon, her mother coffined up in her bed and refusing to rise up out of it — shrouded up in the white sheets and shivering set to quake the foundations of the house and shake the teeth out of her head. Sick sick sick.

Her father: pacing in the kitchen and yelling senseless at the cat — screaming at it to get out of his kitchen. Her father — belly-blown and unshaven and unwashed for days, screaming up the stairs at her mother:

"Get that cat out of the house — if you don't, I'll wring its fucking neck — where's my breakfast?" And then, turning to his daughter, "What're you doing here, you stupid monkey? You're no good for anything." This last bit yelled at her — the small child, child alone, waifish thing, tangled hair and weak, thin with the neglect of years — and so —

This morning like every other summer morning she runs out the back door barefoot across the yard and over the back fence to sit by this little ragged stream and listen to the frogs. To watch twigs float, slow turning down slow currents, and to build a boat out of tree bark and stone it with pebbles to sink it down.

There's no reckoning this. She can't hold in her mind the palish, deadish mother quaking under the sheets, the father stamping down the kitchen floor and yelling — once flinging the cat out the window — the child screaming and running after the furball of fear to pick it up, to clutch it close to her chest, to calm it down, to save it save it save its life, and carry it to the stream to sit with her — but the cat clawed her neck and ran off.

At 2:00 the mother will stumble up into the dim afternoon and creep down the stairs, hooked over the banister, clutching onto it, and shuffle into the kitchen to make coffee. Doesn't eat though. This thing she has won't let her eat. Sick sick sick and dead pale with it, all pale and all shivers.

And the daughter doesn't know what that thing is that is destroying the mother. She sees the flat eyes, the jutted bones, the cast of deep shadow, but can't ask the why of those bones, those shadows.

And she doesn't know the thing that is destroying the father either — she sees him in his rage, but can't imagine the cause or even ask if there is one. It's who he is — this rage — it's all of him — who he's always been and how she's always known him.

And so she makes do for herself, lives on bread and peanut butter that she folds into her pocket, and in the summer, lives the long long day outside and settles in by the old straggle of a stream to watch twigs and bugs float by on the murk, and sit quiet on the grass — removed from that house of hate.

She crouches by the stream and waits with a terror in her belly until she has to go back. To eat. To sleep.

Sundown. Knows the mother will stare at her like she's an urchin come in off the street — those flat deadish eyes under eyelids sunk down, raggish hair, face white. Knows the father might pick her out for his next target — if not the cat, if not the mother, then her.

The willow on the other side grazes the bank. The sun now throwing tree shadows all over, that old fallen tree about a mile up, where it bridges the stream, could cross it and go on through the night, through trees, knock on doors and get taken in somewhere. But can't — the father would get mad. She stands and turns and forces the flats of her feet to drag her back to the house. She looks like the mother now.

And down the years, first scant then fleet, she'll carry all of this with her: sick mother, raging father, and the old wooden house structured up inside her. She'll never get rid of it—every event, every moment of her life will step and shift inside the walls of that house, built up rotten board by rotten board by rotten board within her.

One morning in her thirty-fifth year—in a tiny apartment, no job, no money, the father of her child long gone—she will scream at her own small daughter who's opening the fridge and taking out a plastic cup of peaches—to get the hell out of the kitchen and what does she think she's doing here, and "Get out or I'll throw you out, you stupid monkey— I'll…" She stops there. Stops and stares at her child, sits at the kitchen table, staring at her child, seeing God knows what or who.

She's held hostage in the house. In her memory it is long gone, but inside of her self it will always stand, rotten boards piled up and hoarded up and roofed over within. And she'll always be there inside, standing in the kitchen, small child, child alone, waifish thing, tangled hair and weak, thin with the neglect of years.

WALL OF GLASS

She is sitting in a rocking chair. Alone. Trying to thread a butter knife with a shoelace. On her lap is a brown stuffed rabbit. She tries to understand what it might be doing there.

In the past months, objects in her world have shifted, evolved—a chair has moved from one corner to another, a comb has grown teeth. A bowl melts into a dog's bark. Sometimes the changes are sharp. Sometimes subtle. Sly. Letters in the alphabet no longer worthy of trust. A *j* could be a *q* for instance. In disguise as a *y*.

She rocks back and forth, the butter knife held up to the light in one hand, and the shoelace held up in the other. She must solve this—on her own. If she takes the plastic cap off the string, maybe then it will fit?

Was a time it would fit—but in a larger thing than a needle, boxier, like a small car with no wheels. A thing she used to wear and would lace up herself without her mother's help. And she did it, too!

Where is her mother now? Why isn't she here to help

her — at least to move the bed and the chairs and the dresser back to where they belong.

She rocks faster, holding the butter knife and the shoelace. She looks from one to the other, then puts them down on a small table beside her chair. The table, the chair, the butter knife, the shoelace all shrink into themselves and slink away like thieves in the blight, slipping away into another room.

Where is — ?

Her mother should be here.

There's that colour in the hanging things — like the ones in her bedroom.

And the light is screaming in through the wall, a diffuse light — too bright — a fog and a thickening murk of light seeping in. This light rambunctious to say the least.

This bed in the wrong place, and not hers, nor this chair, nor that picture on the wall — that picture of — a square thing and a yelling roundness that glows all over a floor of glass — no, not quite glass —

It is — outside the room when she looks out before going into the kitchen where her mother is making breakfast — toast and jam — that's it — that glass out there on the ground after a good rain, looks — and she can hear minnows singing or — canaries, and — what is that sound — like a sound at school. Keep an eye on the door. It's closed — must get ready to escape — in case.

That sound, *not* a school sound — more like — she is eight and having her tonsils out, that bing-bong sound down the hall and —

The walls the same colour as the walls in this room, but

not the picture —

The picture of glass.

Or no. Not glass.

She can't smell any toast. Heart beats fast — this bed — this bed is not hers, was never hers, will never be hers. So —

She is — she must be — visiting her friend Katie and her mother in their little apartment on the Rose Valley Road — that's it. This bed is Katie's bed. But where is Katie? And her tennis racket is not here either, so how can they play tennis with no rackets?

She's waiting for her father to pick her up, and Katie — she's gone for a swim — that's it. Lake water, pool water, that colour is: qua qua qua aqua —

That sound — no —

Duck and cover! Don't panic, children! If the bomb drops you must hide under your desk and curl up into a very small ball, and the desk will protect you in the event of a nuclear blast. Miss McFarlane, is that so? Are we safe? For God's sake, Miss McFarlane — please tell us! *Are we safe?*

But where is Father? He must be coming to pick her up now. For this chair not hers — this bed not hers and that picture on the wall — of glass.

The light too strong — draw the skirts across the wind. Light is hurting — oh.

That time on the lake in the boat — oh, the sun dazzled on the water and tossed up handfuls of di…of dy…of dying mountains — each one a treasure. The calm, the quiet of the lake and the call of a canary or a crow or no — a seacall. A seacall cries. Carries a fish.

And her mother on the shore waiting for her to come in with the wind — cover the wind — oh! Waves! So she can make breakfast for her. But where is breakfast? She can't smell any toast, she's hungry, and this bed not hers — it must be — heart beats fast — Katie's?

That bing-bong sound. Grade 6. Recite: "When I was wandering as a crowd…" Duck and cover, children. Now! Are we safe? The bell — but no — this is *not* that sound. It is vanilla ice cream and a sore throat.

Katie. That must be her bed — but where is she? She's gone for a swim in the pool. That colour — that aqua aqua aqua qua qua qua —

Duck! Hands on your head. It is, after all, the end of the world, but your school desks will protect you, children.

"Four crows on a pond. A grass bank beyond."

That's it! *Grass*. The picture — that colour is — grass is green.

The light pouring in now — all lost under the blind sun. Streaking of light — scalding light. Burns.

Here is a small long thing on the table and a rope to go in it. Who left it here? And this piece of shaggy thing with ears.

And where is Mother? Or Father, who is coming to pick her up.

That sound —

No! We are *not* safe! Draw up the — cribbage. The castle, the feudal system, the serf and the Lord's manor and all the knights — those pictures — on horses. Grade 7. Mr. Thomas. He has a beard and is a gypsy. Kind.

Ice cream and a sore throat and Mummy standing beside the hospital bed and — no.

This bed not hers — whose, then, *whose?* And ginger ale with a plastic straw in a grass full of — sip it in, you'll feel better — where is Mother now? Is she alright? *Is she?*

It is — this room — this bed not hers — this chair not hers — that picture on the wall of glass — or no. Not glass.

The light frothing now like waves of the sea — a dense feeling of singing or concussion of light of brightness from the round yelling blind thing in the sky — that — like a baby face or a spoon or the Owl and the Pussycat or no. It was a cow jumped over it.

This rabbit — that's it — not hers — must belong to Katie — oh God! Where *is* Katie? Is she alright? She's been so long away, too long away — she's been swimming in the pool — is she — *is she alright?* That colour that qua qua qua —

That — "I wandered lonely as a crowd..." Mushroom crowd — how do we make ourselves *small*, Miss McFarlane? How do we make ourselves small enough?

Her father is late now and her mother will be waiting for her, breakfast prepared. But she can't smell any toast — not yet. She's hungry.

And what is this — this silver pen and this cotton thread which is as thick as a snake?

The light is a flood now, the ceiling a river, the floor a capsized boat, the bed not hers — a sunken wreck of a boat — eels creeping through like snakes, this rust of light. The chair is a tiger, the picture is a wall of glass and her father — is late. Where is he — is he on the way? *Is he?*

And the door opens and it is — it is — no. It is not her father, not her mother, not Katie. It is not Miss McFarlane or Mr.

Thomas. It's someone she has never seen before, standing there and staring at her, saying, "It's me, Mum," over and over. Standing there, still. With the ocean on her face.

Tell us: *Are we safe?*

THE FRET

The fret had a fight with her — had her nerves in its fists. They were at the ko. It was now the horror of awkward shapes, of certain numbers that appeared to be wrong. It was the dread of losing an umbrella, a sock. The fear of someone's back turning on her, against her — the disdain, the scorn. It was the anxiety of: scissors opening and nothing to cut. The terror of being alone with impossible thoughts: Why did Monica send a picture of a giraffe? What does it mean, a giraffe, does it have some meaning she doesn't know about? It is dread of kk instead of ok, the meaning there obscure and malign. Monica.

It was no fight, no flight, it was cough or jog, it was just painful enough, just nagging enough to wipe out all possibilities and all possible good. It was fear of the flagrant, the unintelligible. Buttons on washing machines, the clatter of rain just before it became hail.

Birds singing at 4:00 in the morning. The number 4 dismissive, almost military. A line in salute. Zeros that stared and marched by the thousands, mob mental. 00000000000000.

Causes were epic, multifarious, protean. She couldn't count them or even recognize them — not before the thing — the fret — showed up. Causeresult so instant it was one thing. Causes multiplied as rats breed, as numbers exponentialize. A fire alarm, a bass guitar, a half-spoken insult hanging in the air, a waft of garbage. Monica. Those who picked through recycling bins dragging along metal carts. What do they want? A typo. The unmitigated horror of subtext. Sarcasm.

When the fret had its fists against her head, her skin turned flagellous, inside out. Muscles plucked at her bones and her gaze rolled white and wall-eyed to the inward dwelling. The sized and the seized and the sunken deep.

The fret stilled her in its stranglehold, thieved away her good mind, scavenged her heart of any feeling that tried to curl up small and harbour there. During the fret, her forward will and the wide seeing of her eyes went blinkered in. Stopped. Then it was: the number 3 deformed, half-fulfilled, tentative and lopsided. The word "minuscule" just a gigantic error of judgement and vision. The act of love a riddle demented. Syncopation, running deprived of forward motion. The gloss of mirrors grotesque. Parsley — the uselessness of it on a plate, exactly like the number 3,830. Useless. Redundant. Green. Embarrassed. The hideous mob mentality of zero. A sneer snaking above a long defiant chin. Monica.

What did she mean when she said that? And then sent the photo of the giraffe, kk.

She tried to reason with herself. Here, self: Remember this. There is a lot to worry about after all. There is. A lot could go wrong. Any number of things. 3,383,000 things. To worry is normal. It is human. It is to be alive. The fumes inside a locked door. No chance of not inhaling. So. Carry on.

Fretting doesn't help, and it doesn't help to know it doesn't help. Keep clam and carry on. No one wants to know about it. Clock it. Zip it. The endless severity, the indifference of zeros.

Crowds. Good God. Crowds. 00000000…

Her entire body was an animal hunted, un-colour-coded, uncamouflaged, exposed to the elementals. To people. To Monica. Hunted by numb objects, ripped by blind circumstance, spurious evidence. Cloth of life torn to shreds, hairline fractures.

Dodging invisible assailants and ruptures within. Lame and limping, belly saturated with a thirst for the predictable, the normal and the quiet.

The fears — they tangled together and held her close to earth, a complex rhizoid system that bound her inward and knotted her down and under, ever tightening its sinewy grips, shooting out new tendrils that snaked around her and strangled her goodwill. A root system interminable, an infinite equation of dread. The terror of: $2x + 3 = x + x + 3$.

The shape of it was: horrific paradox. Monolith tangled. Unrecognizable and fever blue, alive in itself, seeding itself bright in every cell of her body, taking root in every thought that entered her mind. The grief of suspicion, the acid taint of mistrust. Monica. Kk. Subtext. 3.

Now she can't find her pencil. It strikes the core of her as an ur-loss and she will not outlive it.

MAMBOO

Mama, I am in Mamboo. Don't try and find me here. You will never find me here.
It is impossible to find anyone.

I am fine. Please don't send me any more emails. I am fine. To put your restless mind at ease: Again: I am fine.

I have everything I need here:
Small damp white hand towels. Ramen noodles, pad Thai noodles, spaghetti noodles and a hundred other hot meals from a dispensing machine down the hall.
Laundry, even a laundry! I know that will make you happy.

I fold my blue towel—everyone has a complimentary blue towel—and leave it outside my door, and it is picked up, washed and replaced. Just like a real hotel! I think it is there also for identification purposes—ie: it is a microchipped towel and may also be a camera, I'm not sure. Mamboo has a comprehensive surveillance system, you will be glad to know. It makes us feel safe.

The shower is two floors down and I share it with the others like me — the many, many others — I have to book two weeks in advance, sometimes more than that, but I don't mind. I don't need a real shower all the time. You remember how I used to hate the water, how I screamed when I was little and you tried to wash my hair. How you screamed at me. On my floor there is a sink in a corner at the end of the hall for small cleaning and washing and I use that sometimes.

We even have a library here, so you will see now how happy I am. You understand? It is full of all the comics ever made! Row upon row — 40,000! All I do is sign out a copy and take it back to my room to read.

I have been living here three years. It is my home.

My home.

I love living here.

When I walk down the hall to my cubicle, I feel I am in paradise — like I am walking in the green field and under the blue sky of Twelfth Run. The walls in the corridors are even dark blue, but lit from the inside so they glow. And there is a soft blue carpet on every floor. So calm! So peaceful! The walls are cameras, I've heard, but I'm not sure about that.

Sometimes I hear music, but I don't know where it is coming from.

The others love it here as much as I do. They don't speak to me. I never see them, but I know they are happy. I know because this Mamboo is full and there is even a waiting list of thousands to get in! So you see how lucky I am to be here.

It is beautiful.

Beautiful.

I will tell you now how my cubicle is: heavenly, serene and just like being inside an Apex Systems Room in Twelfth Run. It is small, ok? But you know I like to be in small spaces remember when I was little, how I used to hide in the groceries box? And you would have to turn it upside down to get me out! And I would scream, and you would scream.

How is Pachu? Are you feeding him the yellow treats? I hope so.

My cubicle is 9 feet by 3 feet, and it has a widescreen desktop and TV at one end and a big leather chair to sit in. I feel like a real princess in that chair! Bose headphones and a VR mask are attached to it. In that chair I am a pilot, a driver, a hunter, a soldier, an assassin or anything I want to be! There are endless possibilities. As you always said, there are endless possibilities.

At the other end of the room is a mat with its own pillow and blanket. The blanket is a nice peach colour.

The computer screen is flat but has a slight welcoming curve to it, as if it might want to wrap me in a big hug! I love it! Remember how I used to be sad all the time? I'm not sad now. I'm well.

Well. I am so well. You would not recognize me. I am not sad. No. Not ever.

I sometimes chat with my AI if I feel like it, and she answers me and tells me funny things too, like, "Where have you been, Sandra? I've missed you." I say, "I've missed you too." And she says, "Let's get to work!" or "How was dinner? Did you try the falafel?" or "Sandra, you are so funny sometimes, you forgot to fold your towel."

Mama, I have a lot of friends on social, so don't worry about me. I am fine. More than fine.

Please don't try and find me here. You will never find me. I promise you. Here's why:
Mamboo has 168 floors and 38 cubicles on each floor. You see? Every cubicle has someone in it, but you will never see anyone — only sometimes a pair of sandals outside a door or a folded towel. If you leave your cubicle at the same time as someone else, they will close their door quietly and respectfully and wait til you have gone before they come out.

I sleep well in my cubicle. It is quiet. There is no window. I don't have to worry about what is outside. I don't hear traffic. I don't even own a mask! There is no ceiling on the cubicles, so I hear the person in the cubicle next to mine breathing softly at night, and sometimes he snorts or laughs. 😊 Then I wake up thinking he is right next to me, holding me and laughing. And I smile at him.

It is comforting to know I am surrounded by people just like me — people who like manga, who love to be on social and

gram, who love to play Twelfth Run. Many of us do that for many hours in the day. We love to play the game and we love each other.
We love each other. I love everyone here. Everyone.

I am almost certain the person in the cubicle next to me is my partner in Twelfth Run, I could swear he is, but I will never know that. And he will never know that I am his partner. His avatar is the sweetest! It has green hair and a little pig snout! He is always smiling.

Mama, I saw a man in a dark coat yesterday IRL standing at the end of the hallway on the fifth. He looked at me. I think you may have sent him to find me. Is that true?

Please don't send anyone to try and find me. As I told you, it is impossible. No one can find anyone here.

We protect our anonymity. We are unforgiving. Whoever comes to look for us here will die trying to find us. If I see that man again, I will report him.

You asked me in your last email where I hoped to be in five years. I hope to be here, in Mamboo.

You asked me how I can afford to live. I won't answer that question, but give peace to your restless mind, Mama, I do make enough to live on, you don't need to know how, and it is not expensive to live here. I even have enough to get my nails done every week at the salon on the fifth. Right now they are silver and pink.

You asked me again and again and again where I am. Do not ask anymore.

All I can tell you is: I am here, in Mamboo. But I can't say which one or on which continent — just that you would have to cross at least one ocean to get here.

I am happy here.

Happy.

I have never been as happy as I am now.

No one bothers me.

I don't have to speak to anyone, and I don't. I don't have to look at anyone, and I don't. I don't have to suffer anyone looking at me because they don't.

The climate in Mamboo is always comfortable and just right.
The screen is always on.
Wi-Fi is always free.
The games are good.
It is quiet.
I am at peace. I do not worry.

What more could you ask for me, your daughter, Mama, than this? This peace and this happiness?

My life here is a good life.
So do not try to track me down. I will not be found.
Send the man in the coat away. Give him your money and tell him to go home. Please.

And don't ask me about the future, ok, Mama? As if it is something you own and you are giving to me. It is not. I own my future. I created it.

You gave me nothing. And I have built out of this nothing a bright and safe and certain future.

This is my last email to you. If you write to me again, I will not reply.

But rest assured, Mama, I am, at last, happy.

Let me go.

I was your daughter,

I was,

Miriam.

PS: Don't forget to feed Pachu the yellow treats.

LAUGH RIOT

Held himself up for ridicule. Had the right size and look for stand-up. Tall, skinny, long mournful po-face, honk of a nose, thin blond hair, those heavy caterpillar brows, always working themselves into a trauma above round shock-stunned eyes.

Hardly had to speak and people would laugh. He'd just stand there in the spotlight, rub his forehead, twitch his mouth, raise an eyebrow and they'd be off. He'd say a line, and they'd roar with it, the laughs looping around him, lashing his face.

Hated that sound. Loathed it like misery. But this laugh track bought him all he could put his name to: condo in Toronto, a smaller one in L.A., job on an American sitcom, beautiful girlfriend, most coveted parties, never did feel FOMOed. Never did go without. A thing. Had it all.

He studied the way of it, the science — the precision — and got so good he could predict the exact sound of a laugh — whether it would be solid like an egg or ragged at the edges like a dog-gnawed bathmat. Or trailing like worm slime on a sidewalk. He lived the cause, the moment and result of every line.

At home he spent hours listening to recordings of his performances. He collected them, named them, dated them, filed them away. He wanted to find out what caused the laugh — was it the line, the delivery, the tone, the timing, the mood of the audience? What.

After a few years, he stopped listening to the lines and began to hear only the sound of the laugh itself. The caws, the chuckchucks, the hmhummms, the hacks and the hawhaws, the screes and the whoops. The strange nightjugging noise. And he asked that question: Why do people laugh? Other animals don't laugh. Or maybe they do. Maybe chimps do. Maybe hyenas do. Maybe porpoises do.

He sat for hours at his desk, headphones on, analyzing each giggle, shriek and guffaw. At times he could hear a definite rhythm — almost natural like the sea or the wind, depending on the density and the contagion of the laugh.

At other times, when the laugh was not one sound but a mingling of many discordant sounds, he heard nothing but random cacophony. The noise unnerved him — he thought he could hear a message in it. He played some of the laughs backwards. That scared him — the backrushing surge — the way the fadeout crescendoed into hysteria and then suddenly erupted.

He couldn't pull himself away from it — that noise that turned many human beings into a single beast, that noise that was a substitute for the primal scream. It said: We're here on this planet and we don't know why, and our pants keep falling down, and we got spinach in our teeth, we are all knock knees and anxiety and our hair is falling out, and we trip over our ankles as we cartwheel into the grave, and our skin is falling down and it's a fucking joke all of it and we hate this joke and we hate you for telling us this joke.

And so: We open our mouths. Not to laugh. No.

The better he got at hooking the laughs, the more he hated the noise and the faces behind the noise. He could see the people in the first couple of rows, their faces caught in the half-glow. He could see them gnashing their teeth. They wanted to take a bite out of his arm and chew up his bones.

He saw it, he heard it. His hatred and fear of them became so hot it turned his face red and that made them laugh even more. As he spoke his lines, the cold fear sweat rolled off him, he muttered, he lost focus, he pictured a lady in the front row with a fish fork in her forehead, a business type with toothpicks in his eyes.

He began to forget his lines, replacing them with gibberish — or the lines would turn on him and sucker punch him in the face. But his fumbling made no difference. They laughed just as loud as before. He could do no wrong.

One night he trashed all his jokes and stood there for two whole minutes, saying nothing. He scratched his head and they went wild. Thought it was hysterical. He told them what he ate for lunch. They chuckled at the lettuce, convulsed at the pickle. His hatred was grinding him up inside. He knew he had to put an end to it. It was over.

The last night of his career, he walked out onto the stage knowing this was it. He cracked a few old one-liners, they laughed and smashed their hands together. He tried a new line: How do you know when you're in trouble? When you look in the mirror and your reflection doesn't bother to show up. Not that funny. Not at all funny. But they loved it. Laughed a convention. And that's when he tipped. Couldn't resist.

He started in: a monologue. A harangue. A hectoring of fear and hatred that had built up in him over the past eight years. "I despise all of you," he began. "You're all idiots. You're all losers. You have no idea who you are or what you are, you're all cheap merch-addicted, candy-crazed zombies. That's all I have to say. Get out of here and get lost. Go back to your zombie caves…"

He went on like this for twenty minutes. After every line, the audience laughed. They roared, they clapped, they whistled. It was yukyuk haha all the way down. His best performance. The more he berated them, the louder they laughed. They adored it.

When he finally said, "I quit," and stepped down off the stage and made his way to the front door of the club, they all stood up as one and gave him a standing ovation.

They turned and watched him as he pushed his way through the crowd. They cheered, pumped their fists in the air, stamped their feet, called his name.

Finally, he got to the door. They blocked it. He turned to face them. They began to tap him lightly on the shoulder.

TRACKLESS

Traction traction these valleys of sand this journey for a fool. A fool cast out. Machine coughing and sinking in the granular centuries. This desert red and once holy land now firing up to split tongues of heat scarring the sky in wavering sheets and shimmers of light. Ashes of fire falling. Wheels on the way to melting sinking sinking and downthrusting wheels. No track. Trackless sand sand and red sand, white sky furrowing with troughs and tongues of white blazing heat. Unbearable weight of sky and light. Red dust. White sky ungiven land, land untouched, rejected and thrown back before the act, the act of creation.

Starting point:
Coordinates:
Destination:

No one been here before this, before this journey. Fool. Forward motion sensation only — false chink of light — false. False gleam of a lying light, dying spark, all promise and no give, no gift of light. Machine gasps on fumes of gas, fuming gas and choking red sand red sand white sky. Cheat of light.

Cheat. Bastard false gleam of light.

  Heat illusions up ahead: camels

        elephants

              swarms of gnats

                      storm c.ouds. Impossible to tell.

                                Clouds.

Intractable surface, shifting ground of granular centuries. White sky and clouds of — a

Engine cough.

Rest a moment. Stop. Nowhere now but — at

At the end of this sandscape, this shift and roll, over these dunes maybe on the other side of the s.orm dunes. Storm. And beyond the red rage of mountains raging out red in the white sun intractable sky far off far off. Ok. somewhere beyond in that place you — Listen. Listen:

You heard of it as a village — it was called — it had a name — n.me. Name. or as a moveable marketplace with stalls of balsa wood loosely framed and shadowed in the muted light. Stalls where fish and mangoes and bright fabrics were sold, where fountains plashed in cobbled squares and fresh water ran free and sweet to the tongue. Dark sleek bottles of fine wine in the evening. Necessary rest. Caesura. Pause. The sun set, the light shifting down and dozing down and dreaming down into the consoling dark the cool cool siege of night. Fermata. This is:

How you heard of it long ago. You heard its name, as if something real. As if. You heard it was real and of a reliable substance. Named and therefore is. N.med. And so you you wrestled everything together — every scrap and every thread and every trinket and every stick and sold it all for this:

This old beaten-down, gas-choked, flame-throwing machine so you could take this so-named: blessed journey. Lost, abandoned, ill-intentioned. False. Journey for a fool. This journey you thought. Thou.ht. was so sanctioned and so true. Sanctioned by "God", sanctioned by a bald rabbi reciting Kaddish, by a father who studied the law, by a grandfather with white hair, of terrifying stature, scholar who knew, who knew the law, professing this much: that such a journey would be worth it. Fool. You heard of it, you heard it spoken of but that means nothing. It was all gone long ago. Taken away down miles of track. Wheels turning in the night. Track of the sun. Inscribed and recorded recorded to death.

Gone.

Still.

To find this other place beyond the red sand white sky furrowing into troughs and tongues of heat, ashes of fire, beyond the red raging mountains. You think you haven't seen this? You've seen it. This small village or market with stalls of balsa wood, loosely framed, the glitter of fish scales the bright willowing fabrics luffing and snapping in a clear soprano of a breeze. You think you haven't seen this? You've seen this.

Machine gasping on fumes now, now veering side to side. List one way. List the other way. Wheels sinking in sand. Sinking and down-thrusting engine. Trackless. Impossible tilt. Hold tight to the wheel. Hard to keep it steady in the shift, the roll and drift, the swallow and valley of sand sand red sand white sky furrowing keep the balance.

Ba a a a lance. Side to side. Impossible veer to the right and to the left. Un-nameable angle.

It had a name it was called. You heard it once as something nameable and real. A village well-loved, a market.

Keep the thing upright and moving forward move it forward even if forward is no such thing. Only a hope. A senseless hope, all motion is hope, all hope is senseless. Journey of a fool. False and sinking in granular centuries red sand red sand white sky. Hope less journey of a fool. But still more: a hope.

A sensation. Hold on to that: the sensation only: journey of a fool: sensation of a journey. Sensation only

Starting point:

Coordinates:

Destination:

Drive to it all the same, all the same drive on drive on drive forward the forward motion through the sand red sand white sky furrowing in shimmers of heat—to a distant place, its name—its name—remember it. The sensation of the forward motion down-thrusting engine the driving through—sensation only. False. Unnamed. Only a feeling of movement, a false feeling of movement, and the gleam of it in your eye. Eye of glass. Your eye of glass.

UPDRAFT

I got taken up by a tornado. It was remarkably still in there.
"No, I'm alright," I said to my brother.
A child's shoe flew by.

PANIC ROOM

Indwelling here, cloistered in and suffocating under a heavy haze of microscopic matter — zigzagging blind and chaotic. Moth patterns flicker against a dim-lit wall. In this room, a whole winter of distress, with its cold, with its damp. The no window and the no door of it.

Hallucinate. Yes. Why not — pierce through the haze to another light-filled place — filaments and curls of white-petalled gardenias, level beams of light that irradiate wide meadows and suffuse the air with calm. Maintain a dull-hooved plod, the steady tread of slow comfort under the grazing sun. Unseen. Unheard of and without will. Calm and dwelling in gentle sunlit lands, laced and purled in green, green days, green trees, the fine withering of shadow in the green-lit dawn. Moth soft and wheeling round slow. Dream this. Until it is real and vision bright.

But no — in a snap: fled. A single thought bolts, and the haze rushes in and smudges the whole vision to a flat stubborn grey. White-walled in this room. This is the real and the endless terminal — this prisoneiric of disquiet, building fast monuments to fear. No chance of escape. Thoughts dizzying round in here, storm-driven, static. Go for the door, no door. Go for the window, no window. Go for the floor. Flatten. Nowhere to hide from it.

Begging for release when release is not possible. Walled in by distress and hemmed in by the white walls. And this is just the problem: the smallness of the ever-diminishing space.

Forward motion nothing but a vicious trick of the light. And the microscopics of distress, whizzing and shuddering round in here like clouds of gnats. In this room—safe from the outside but prey to whatever is in here, unknown and unguessed at. The kinetics of chaos whip and spin to frenzied and chthonic defeat.

Dream. Hallucinate. Try. Your only hope—see: another distant land of outdwelling spaces, flat meadows of saturate green, the kind and open sky, a generous canopy of blue, streams of filtered light above the wide witnessing fields of wheat, golden and warm in their upward sway. Vast oceans of phosphorescent glow.

Escape from this room and out to a redemption in all its young finery, calibrations of light, attending flutes, child-dreamed beasts from ancient pages—mock turtles and centaurs who sit with you in the peace and in the light. A flurry of apple blossoms and a breezing of birds above the rolling green.

No chance.

Dream what you will, it will not be strong enough to beat down the real. Distress has its solid way, the four white walls around you. Concrete is cruel; it does not give. You are trapped here. In this smallest of dark rooms. Go on. Pound your fists against the horizons of white, if you will. But the room itself is telling you this: There is no beyond. There is only here, and only this room.

This wall and this wall and this wall and this wall.

THE WEAK

The trembling the fearblind and faint of pulse the light-boned cowering back-turning head-bowing sniveling and whimpering in the dark, fearstunned by the dark fidget-cringing skullduggering mange-eaten sallow-skinned brine-whingeing brow-frowning and teeth-grinding hand-wringing arm-twisting conniving vicious-eyed malignant-willed. base. lying trodden underfoot to rank obedience obsequious gut-wretched wrung to the bone feral-hearted promise-spewing tooth-gapped poison ugly child-cheating thieving cursing god-defiant loveless in a white-tiled room professing dancing round soaked and saturated to the marrow with falsehood and pretense. homeless. tarp-dwelling piss-drenched reeking and ever unredeemed wind-whipped and forsaken in the sand-shifting desert spirit-sunk. These. The weak. The fearful. The threadbare of will who neither stand nor serve: we also struggle also wish to live.

BURN HECTIC

It begins at five. At all other times under control, working hard at the school, flat-heeled and sensible, well-liked, her opinion often sought and given, an upstanding member of society. Until five. Then the betting shuts down, the pawn shops close, all trading ceases on the TSX. Then it begins. One drink, and another and another until the blur dissolves the world into a liquid murk. She observes it from a distance with a canny disdain. Swills the drink down, and refills and refills until the liquid seeps into the hollows within, dark spaces torn by sharp stalagmites, and slippery with the ooze of green lichen.

The drink dazzles those spaces with a ginnish vibrancy—a colour that hasn't been named yet—a whole world of light can be built out of it, she knows, and this world peopled by laughing rebels who rampage and destroy, carve out of the depths kinetic structures which they then tear down with glee and a burning will—an enthusiasm she hasn't seen in herself for many years, if ever. A wild and sinning joy infuses her and drowns the emptiness with a malignant feverish red, first blood of the hunt. Rebels tear down monuments of autocrats, crush old stone to powder, demolish the barricades and break all in their path, the imperial rule in flames.

She watches this hive of chaos and conflagration and drinks again, yet another glass as gangs of thugs roam hectic through the darkness, light fires that flame up high and burn effigies of all her past loves and losses—a man she once knew and loved, her mother dying endlessly within, and a watching child—her witnessing and helpless self. All, all going up in a panic of flames—a terrifying sadness to rejoice at. A wondrous annihilation.

The world outside pales to whitish mist, she sees it from far far away now. Inside, a catastrophe of flames burns to high heat and melts the substance of feeling to a tiny mercurial drop—all her sorrow, regret, pain, remembrances—gone. Only a waft of smoke remains as she peers out at the distant world, and as the world glances back at her, askance. No pity, no condemnation either, just the white silence of a world given up on her, and within, a self drained of all that once was, drained to the last drop, and the dregs burnt up to a white-hot indifference.

YELLOWCAKE

Green bile hypes him up until he would look lovingly on the deepest sin. And he would mince words with meat cleavers, and hack about in his Gobi mind for some meaning of any fury-buried thing, whether vegetable, mineral or damned animal, god or goddess; in his mind he lives, searching.

If the moment feels right he will beat the daylights and the nightlights out of his beloveds, and then gallon up his noxious fuming in rusted tanks, and mint coins of slander and puke; the thick-wadded yellowcake stashed deepaway, as he fears the petty purview of even the most casual visitors. Hide it, hide it, cool and clammy in the downsinging earth, so no blindy eyes can see the loathing fumes that seethe and flicker there. Only a spark fusing, no clear intention yet. Not yet.

Driven, bile-minded, ploughing inward, ever inward where brooding sepsis and fear root.

In the begin years, dadadada flailed the thwacker at this tiny-aged boy and put the dread of slasher-kills in him, even then, at the mewling age of a tiny walloped babe in harm's way.

It started then. It grew after, down the year-to-year, in basement silence, hatching out Guy Fawkesish plots and scribbling Gothic incendiaries in the dark.

And now, so, now, now in this no-jesting moment, what could turn ever so easy on a wing flutter, given a kind word or two, does not. Does not, as no kind words come forth.

Now, the ancient terror and acid-eating fear singes the Gobi of his mind and turns, spiral-dusting, into whipper-whorls and toronadoes of hate. And he feels it deep in his ancestor bones and he loves it to the oblivion of love and he turns the yellowcake of it over and over again in his fisties, feeling he is well worn to it, well used to it, and the spinning whorls call to him oh so lovingly in aching harmonies and even cheeky-pie whistles.

And he's hidden his hate away so deep in the whingeing world that no one can see it but himself only, and he would love it til the world's end, and would create that world's end just to howl in full-throttled voice the love he feels for the yellowcake feel of it, and the blue-black danger of it, the thrust and centrifugal force of it and the sear-blinding panic of it.

And while you wait for your clipper-handed hair fashionista or sip, froth-minded and fair-willed, on a Frappacinnamingo and smile at your fair-browed barista, he grows sallow and greenier in his Gobi mind, as he sees no shining future like your very own one, no condo at the lakefront, and no Pomeranian panting pretty-wise down the street, no lunch out at the Flying High Nines under the rainbow-casting chandeliers, not even a bank account to speak of or a job in the offing. There is none of that for him. It is all yours, all of it.

And the one thought you have: you do not want him in it, here in your camomile, peach and heavenly life, you do not want to hear of his knife-wielding thoughts and his greeny gangrened imaginings. And you cannot lay a babyfatted finger on his pain, his blood-gushing wounds. Your eyes go cataractic white when you so much as tip your mind towards a thought of him. And if you catch a glimpse of him, you cover your blindy eyes with the white gauze. Then you turn your back on him, on his despair and on his unsounded need.

And while you rollock and roll and bathe luscious in the melanomic sun and go slobbery in sentiment as you sip cool wine in the cool leather of your Silver Ghosts and Phantom limos and Silver Seraphim, he is watching you and will not take his eyes off you.

And now his intents get to high heat and fire to crystal as he reaches, open-fisted, for the yellowcake.

BLACK WATER

Black milk of daybreak we drink it at sundown
we drink it at noon in the morning we drink it at night
we drink it and we drink it
PAUL CELAN, "DEATH FUGUE"

It started this morning, no big deal, now it is. I turned on the tap in the bath for a shower—wanted the water to drench clean the cant and rave of the night, the shock of dawn. Again, no sleep. Turned on the tap, ready to put my head right under that clean slam of water, before flipping the switch and transforming the frack into a stream of cleansing rain, and with it: hope of all hopes: wake me up, please just wake me up.

Turned the tap to full blast. Water jetted out clean. Then, next minute, turned black—pure black. No smell, no change in viscosity or density. Black pooled round in the tub and eddied down the drain.

Without the shower, went to work. I work in a law office downtown. The morning was catatonically normal, and the afternoon just the same. Always, around three, I lose the thread. What I mean is: I lose the thread of what I'm doing. It's not just fatigue, it's—oh, what am I doing here really? Earning money? For what? To pay my rent so I can get up tomorrow and earn more money to pay my rent? And that malicious circle starts eating its own tail until the space it circumscribes begins to shrink. And if I'm tired anyway, then the minutes blur under the light and the walls stretch away from me, and my fingers don't work on the keyboard—they just lie like uncooked sausages stuck to the ends of my hands. I don't answer messages I should, and I sit in front of the screen and stare, hoping I don't get noticed.

And that's what it was this afternoon, at three exact, I lost the thread, and the work I was doing became moot, became one big question: What is the square root of a cat, exactly? The screen splintered into magnetic fodder, words on the page flatlined into black strips against doc white. And what was that? What was that at the edge of the page? Nothing good.

The spooks from last night—a smiling girl—her golden hair—shards of glass, train tracks, ashes, ax-broken spines—began to rise up and dance in the pit that was my head. I had to get up, get away from my desk. I'll get a drink, I thought.

I get up from my desk and go to the office kitchen. Turn on the tap. The water rushes out—then goes black. Again black. Here, as there. No difference—only more shocking here—here, where nothing is ever out of place, nothing ever misspoken, nothing ever misused. Order triumphs every single day and productivity soars. Yes, everything was normal here, no matter what was happening outside or at home.

The office was my kind sanctuary—until this afternoon.

In the office kitchen, I filled a glass with the black water, held it, took it back to my desk. I sat looking at it, then drank it down. I drank it, I drank the black. It slipped and snaked down into me and curled up in my stomach. There was no taste to it, none. I drank it all down. Had no reaction. I thought it might scorch my intestines but I was wrong. Nothing unusual happened. I can live with this, I thought.

At 4:00, Amber, the office manager, sent me home. "You look awful," she said.

"I am not unwell," I said.

"Go on home and get some rest," she said.

And here I am, sitting at my kitchen table, "getting some rest". Hungry as hell, would boil an egg if I dared, but I won't—won't turn the tap on. I have sleeping pills. I'll take two, swallow them with juice, and they will pitch me into nightmares that are at least recognizable.

I'm getting hungrier, thirstier, and I can feel the black water in my belly begin to curdle and split and slowly leach out through the walls of my intestines. Still no reaction. And if I had one—pain or nausea—what then? No doctor can diagnose this. There's no cure for this. There never was.

The light is going outside my window, no big deal, it's dusk and that's what happens at dusk. But in my belly I can feel the black water rise, drift out to my skin, then seep out through my pores. It floats away from my body in ribbons, I see it as smoke, as an enduring world of black smoke and the smoke whispers out through the kitchen window and dissolves in the dark of night, and the night—the always night — presses its back up against the window, it wants to get in, and in my belly I can feel the black water rising up to meet it, rising up, then resting back down, and pooling, and rising up again, and sinking down, breathing as I breathe. Becoming smoke.

(SHE SPEAKS IN A QUIET VOICE)

For Sarah Kane

Erosion incurs a high cost. Leaving incurs none. Stay and endure the slow burn or give it over. The choice not mine but yours. So speak. I do know you after all. You visited years ago. You spoke to me then, why not now?

Look: over there: it trails behind it the sigh and rush of a long silk train. Whispers to the shades around. Crooks a finger, winks. A carrion clutch of feral cats roams hectic round this figure, all of them bone, bloody and hacked. This petty demon a friend of yours? A fair imitation, but it doesn't fool me. You and you and only you and you alone are the real, the breathing, the dying thing.

You were so eloquent once. So ringing and so true. You spoke to me in amber tones. You camped with me, curled up beside me, breathed with me and as I slept, you whispered each step of your careful instructions. In the morning I wiped the sleep from my eyes and knew the sin, the how of it and of everything.

But you won't speak to me now. You've gone sullen and still, and even if I listen close there is no whisper from you, no murmur, no hum.

Why must I wait? Is the reckoning askew? An unpaid debt, a grievance unanswered, an apology missed? These aren't arguments; deflections only. The act itself dissolves all debt by reason of absence of agency by reason of absence.

As I wait for you to speak, I hear the talk of others around: the breezing on and banter, trade of quips and anecdotes, the: I think you should see this, and the: Why not do this? and the: Why did you think this when clearly it is that? And didn't you know? And I heard this. And martinis, klieg lights, riff-raff, holograms, Christmas lights, words, fractals, the whine of complaint, Norwegian fjords. The endless drag of talk and talk will not end. Not without you.

So speak.

You close up your arms in blue shadow. Jaws clamp shut. Back now turned.

Look: the colour's bled out here to slate grey, metallic disc of the sun and long shadows leaching colour like blood. It's all sunk flat into the dull monochromic. And the more hours, the more grey, the more grey the more grey, and so on and on and on

Why wait until movement is no longer possible, until pain snakes itself around the will to breathe? Until stumbling purblind from bed to kitchen is an unnameable torture? Until aloneness wrestles solitude to the floor and throttles it? Until sleep shatters into a cataract of knives? And until ancient resentments hunt and rove like packs of hyenas under the pale stare of the moon? Why wait.

Why?

For *that*?

No.

I'd rather go with You. You who are kaleidoscopic. Brilliant. Vibrant blue, lightning quick. Vivacious, luminescent and a perfect conversationalist, when you want to be.

So. Speak.

In blue shadow, I see you turn now to face me. I step towards you, you are smiling, and your eyes darken with knowing, with caring. You reach out your hand to me. I take another step.

I'm listening.

COME BACK & NO DON'T

Send me away if you want it's your risk not mine. But if you do send me off you better know what you're doing you better think this one through rightways and leftways and downways and upways and backwards and forwards and every which way. every angle. Just saying. Think this one out. & see,

See: here's the thing:

Send me away and I'll come back anyways. & here's another thing:

If I come back it might be as something you don't want to see with the hahahaha writ all over my face and the joke'll be on you — on your face, miss happy face, miss 'I don't care cos you don't exist anyway', miss 'I'll carry on without you just fine & be best I can be on my own with you gone. and never were anyway'.

Not sonotso not so. Snot nose. I always was. & I always was with you @home with you. Right here @on the range where the deer and whatevertheotherthingis roam. Or some such. You listening? You all ears right now, cos you never bothered to listen before—so I'm: *just shocked!!! just stunned!!!* By the simple fact that right now you do seem to be listening. & are attentive. But are you? *Are you??*

Is this a ruse??? Nonononono, *ma cherie, mein Liebeskind, meine herrliche, breitweise Blume*:: I think not. Ithink notsonot so. I do ins Herz believe you *are* listening to me:

So here it is: straight from the old cow's mouth:

(and if this is a ruse and if you're not listening well then its all your fault what is going to happen & none of my doing my dearmydear, mydarling *kleines Liebeskind*. Not my fault.) 😊

So here it is as you wait with baited breath. *(Not* a spelling mistake. We'll talk about that later.)

Exclude me like you've always done—just u continue to do that—& u exclude the thing u know nothing of. Since u never even bothered to look. U-turn away. Because I am the u of u u don't want to see.

And you know what they say about the things youdon 'tseecan'tseedon'twanttosee. Those things. They are please god they are the very things that come back at you. And bite. Wahhhhp! They bite on you with the fangs out and the jaw locked in and those things you know they hang on to you with the lockjawlocked until, *mein liebes Kind*, well what, *ich meine,* is that they don't let go they *fassen fest* and they hang on until you go necrotic your fingers flacken & blacken & fall off & the arm must be amputated at once. All of it and the other one too while we're at it. nonononono in nowise, *ma cherie*, we do not have any anesthetic. We sold it all and anyways is too expensive for the likes of you. Sososososo.

You see? It will be painful. That's it: well *hier* is the point. in one short line:

———————

The thing you don'tsee will come back as the thing you don'twanttosee.

& that's me: that's me: that's just me. Hi. Howyadoin? Still all ears? Glad to hear it miss happy face 😊 god that really does look like you. Mores the pity.

Send me away and soon *je reviens*, to sting you in the back & cataract your old eyes, and pour slop over your entire memories and twist your flatfoot gait into a crooked lockstep.

It wont take much to do all of this I promise you, miss *hold und schön und rein*.

U have no idea how easy it will be.

Seeseesee misssissy: its just this:

If you send me away again, I will come back and destroy you in an instant. Are we *aneinandervorbeireden?* (look it up) Or are you truly listening? You don't have to answer. But *hier* is what I want to say, *ich meine*:

Takemein. As I am. Don't shut me out. Let me speak mysay and say whatevershitiwant. And however.

Hold me in the

> Deepest part of your *Herz* in there
> where is darkest dunnest smoke of hell
> where nothing bleeds and all is listening and eyes
> so far within so far you never knew it even ever was
> but truly has always been
> hold me there hold me there

embrace theworstofwhoyouareofwhoiam.

& if you dont, I wont be held responsible.
No I wont. Not my fault.
So whats it to be? Im waiting for your decision.
& I can only advise you:

> Think it through before you naysay or yaysay.
> Think it through carefully.

I mean, *ich meine*, I can't tell you what will happen *exactly* if your answer is no, but ill wager my little *Steinleben* in Bitcoin that it wont be good. (and that's another thing: pay that back. You got 50 is now worth 600)

(and the thing with your breath: it smells like a possum died in your mouth. So do something about it for jesus's sake.)

So I'm sitting back here waiting outside for your response and it better be good the lord it better be. So whatsittobe? Whatsittobe? Whatsit? Whatsit? Miss happyface 😊 and growsome hairwhileyouratit.

Well?

RENTER

got home late yesterday. My landlord and his wife were in my apartment. They had an old camera set up in the front room like the ones used in the 1920s, with a tripod and a big black cloth. In the corner was a silver umbrella to reflect light and two huge spotlights on stands. They were discussing the angle of the umbrella. "What's going on?" I said. They didn't even look at me. Acted as if they didn't hear me.

> I went into my bedroom, I thought I could just close my door and wait until they left. There, sitting on the bed was — an electrician, wearing a tool belt, a white helmet and blue overalls. He was just — sitting on my bed gazing at the wall, his elbows on his knees. He was a small man with scruffy back hair sticking out all over and a dark look to him as if he'd been through some terrible trauma and never recovered. He glanced at me when I came in. His eyes were black and flat. There was no expression in them — not the slightest

surprise.

"Have to fix this," he said, but didn't move.

"Fix what?" I said.

He didn't answer. He bowed his head low over his knees like he was exhausted just sitting there.

"You have to get out of here," I said.

"This is my room. You have to get out now."

He looked at me then as if I was an intruder and had no right to be there. He had big construction boots on, unlaced.

I heard footsteps on the stairs.

Six people came tramping up into my apartment, chatting and laughing.

I had no idea who they were.

There was a mother, a father, maybe a sister or a friend and three children.

All of them marched right past me and into the front room.

My landlord and his wife were still in there discussing the location and angle of the umbrella. They were shifting the lights round, pushing my furniture to the edges of the room. Eight people were in there now! Milling about and chatting, like it was some kind of convention.

I went into the kitchen and closed the door.
Sitting at the kitchen table was an old woman I didn't know. She had all my cutlery and glasses and plates laid out on the table in front of her. I grabbed some forks and put them back into the

drawer, but she got up, took them right back
out again, and put them all back on the table
in a neat row.

> I went back into the bedroom. That man — the
> electrician — was still sitting on my bed, still
> staring at the wall, nodding now, as if he
> knew what to do. "I'll fix it," he kept saying,
> but he never got up off the bed.

>> I locked myself in the
>> bathroom and sat on the
>> floor. I would live in here
>> if I had to. There was
>> nowhere else to go.
>> Then I heard humming.
>> I pulled back the shower
>> curtain. Sitting in my
>> empty bathtub was a
>> girl, about eleven years
>> old. She was dressed in an
>> orange party dress and
>> she was sliding a bottle of
>> shampoo — my shampoo —
>> back and forth on the
>> bottom of the tub.
>> This is unacceptable,"
>> I said to her, but she just
>> kept on humming
>> and sliding.

I went back into the bedroom and said the same thing to the electrician. I was about to go into the front room and complain to my landlord about all of this when I heard glass smashing from the kitchen.

                                                            I
                                             didn't
                                               dare
                                             look.

YOU   BODY

You wake up. Yawn. A long, drawn-out yawn from deep inside. Sleepy eyes, tousled hair. You stretch. This skin, this flesh, this you.

Your body is you. In your scant eleven years on this earth—you've never questioned it. Never had to. It carries your spirit inside, and you carry it in your small sturdy shoulders, your spine.

The feel of it is this, isn't it: small and rickety, tentative as a foal as you step out onto a cold stone floor from a warm bed. Born into the day. It is early yet.

You swim in the fresh lake water. Waves course over you. You swim like a creature made of water. Inside you feel an aliveness, a dolphin spirit, and you own the breath and the joy of it, the triumph—to be alive inside your body—imagine—this living, tactile, fluid form that you have and that you are. Your stick legs, knock-kneed, kick up tiny storms as your own life energy ripples out from you and into the water around you. Gift to gift. You revel in the command of body—you spirit it into movement.

At times it turns and plays tricks on you — those burned fingers, that swollen toe — but pain can't hold it back. You dance to the measure of body, and its music is always with you. Cold after the swim, you wrap its shivers in a thick white towel, plunging it into a new warmth as your body plunges you into new joy, blue lips and all.

You are onewithbody, spiritlife, sweet entanglement of force and form — heart and mind cleaving to body and body cleaving to heart and mind. Continual embrace. Ecstatic. You run barefoot up the lawn cloaked in your white towel, the gulls calling and soaring above. You and no one else — in all your innocence and trust — you alone own this body. It is yours.

No one told you it can be taken away — that it is yours only by the consent of others. Even the idea of this is impossible to you. And so, blithe to the danger that would rob you of this body, this life, you run — eternally in this moment — your life stopped here — up a green lawn wrapped in a thick towel.

You, with your belly full now of strawberry jam and toast and Tiger Tail ice cream, with a gap-tooth and a foolish grin across your face — you won't even know when it happens.

Brutal. Sudden.

You don't see the danger. Of course you don't. For you, danger is green, dragon-huge, with shiny scales and long sharp fangs — danger doesn't look like this: a gentle, pale old man in black-rimmed glasses, who smiles and gives you plastic horses with legs that bend, blue candy floss, trips to the zoo, rides on the Ferris wheel. An old and innocent man — innocent because he is a creature like you — this is the trust, isn't it: that he inhabits his body and mind the same way you inhabit yours. And as you honour the spiritlife of others, you know that they must do the same, and honour your own. You never dream that another living being would want to take your body away from you.

And so, this body, this life of eleven years on this earth, in blue shorts and a red- and yellow-striped T-shirt, is easily taken from you.

Brutal. Violent.

The man in his body steals it away.

You go on. Body is still there, it moves, it breathes, but it is no longer yours. It belongs to some thing else. It is: Some. Other. Thing. Dissonant. Remote.

You go on. But your spirit leaves you. Your joy and your sacred trust. You walk by the shore of the lake, eyes cast down to the shifting sand, stumbling by the water, wading diffident in the shallows.

He has left you with this: flesh poisoned to the marrow, sewn up with a decay that feeds itself through you over the years and over the years and over and down the years. And this: a silent heart, a mind riven with distortion, and the rotten will to die — it is a will that never leaves you, a will that has usurped the life you once were, a will that was once a child in the waves and a dolphin spirit.

You are you   body.

THAT OLD LIFE

I got up and saw my whole damn life. It wasn't what you'd think—it wasn't like a series of events flashing before my eyes, moment by livid moment. No. It wasn't even in front of me. It was behind me. Following me.

I went through the regular and indeterminate motions of the day—motions I have long since lost touch with. These routines are meaningless now, but I still go through them because you know. You know—you do know, right? I have to. What else can I do?

But there it was, whatever I did. Following me. I took a shower and it was peering at me over the edge of the tub around the back of the shower curtain. I am nothing to look at, that's for certain, but it looked horrified peering at me like that. Horrified. I was insulted and got dressed—fast—because all this was shameful, shameful—the gall—and then it was hanging *upside down* outside my window, like a jerk—just clownishly showing off, trying to impress me. Waggling its fingers in its ears.

When I had breakfast—which is always the same—one

soft-boiled egg on two pieces of toast and corn flakes, it had the nerve to smash the shell on my egg into tiny fragments so I had to peel the pieces off, one by one. Which I did. And then it fisted my egg into the plate! The outrage!

On my way to work it walked behind me, humming the Marseillaise, (the Marseillaise!), like some teenage goof in flat shoes, sweats and a go-find-me floppy hat. Waddling, waddling behind me, dropping back, then bounding freakishly ahead to keep up, or nosing ahead of me only to look back at me and wink!

I can't say exactly what it looked like — it was just my old life after all. Indeterminate, vague. At first glance, full of direction and verve, but then in the harsh light of the sun, showing its true self and turning out to be puffed up, bloated and full of nothing too much, turning this way and then that. Lost. Until it started following me. The bastard.

It kept getting closer. I walked and it jogged up behind me, or waddled, puffing and wheezing. It was, I have to say it — grievously overweight, saggy and floppy, but still capable of a bound here and there at odd moments. A freakish bound as if to say "Ha!" like those obese people who are surprisingly light on their feet when they dance. And then people say, "Who would have believed they could do that??"

This went on for some time. It got right up close to me, that old life, that old bounder, that old gas heap of a life. And I could see out of the corner of my eye — it had dreadlocks down to its feet and trailing on the ground. Dreads! First thing I would do if I could catch the pig is cut all those off.

That old life, it crept right up behind me when I wasn't

ready for it. A plague and an insult, it wouldn't go away.

It hooked its arm in mine. And then it started to whisper in my ear. A lot of questions. It said, "Huh? Huh? Huh? How are you doing? What are you now? Well? What's going on? What's up? Having done what you have and haven't done, what do you believe about it all? What are you now? What do you think of me, eh? Happy to see me? Eh? Happy? Eh?"

And it just kept whispering that in my right ear as I was walking to work. Over and over again. Little puffs of wind in my ear. It was making me crazy.

I tried to disengage my arm, but it would have none of it. It clung on to me for dear life. For its dear self. The gall! Good God! The nerve! At this time in the morning, too.

"Shut up!" I said and turned to slap it in its pasty insolent face. "Shut up and go away."

"You go first."

"I'm not going anywhere. I'm going to work."

And then it grinned at me, with mouldy teeth and a bloated, air-filled face, and glassy black eyes. Obsidian glare. Eyes that could neither see out nor see in.

The belly bloat was stunning. You could tell it was all air. Which would explain its ability to bound like that—freakishly—and to hang upside down outside my window. Defying gravity—absenting gravity, you could say—that damn old life, bounding listless and aimless and rot-filled, brittle like glass and windblown every which way, full of harm and full of guile.

And now following me, following me every waking hour until at night it lies down beside me and invents a whole catastrophe of dreams and drummed-up chaos. Child. Joker. Trickster. Dream-stuffed and hopped up on hope. Good God! The gall!

If it's still here tomorrow when I wake up, I'll let it know what I think of it. I'll wring its neck.

BONE BY BONE

And I'm sitting in this restaurant and it is a horrible place — the last one of its name and kind in the city — the decor hasn't been changed in thirty years — the brown plastic tables and the pale brown walls — and the menu in its brown plastic cover hasn't changed in thirty years either, that's clear. I'm here because I'm hungry and there's nowhere else to go along this stretch.

I'm trying to eat a piece of stale gelatinous cherry pie. Its guts are bright red, and the crust is not a crust — it's a scab. I can't even swallow it. And there's a picture on the wall above me of a Jesus in blue and white robes with yellow hair and a fiendish sly grin on his face and he's pointing upwards for God's sake — upwards — in a place like this!

At the table beside me, there's a thin old man in a thin grey suit that is three sizes too big for him. His hair is thin. He's sallow and pale at the same time and yellow like bile is yellow — that's what shines through the pallor on this gentleman. And he is sitting there drinking a cup of coffee from a forty-year-old white coffee cup. And does he belong here!

He belongs here just like I belong here.

And he turns and looks at me with his pale grey eyes that are—thin eyes—and he says this to me: no introduction, no small talk, this is what he says:

"Two days ago I'm sitting on the can. I'm sitting there and it's all coming out of me—everything—the altogether whatever is in there and who knows what that is, I mean who *really* knows—and it's all over the toilet seat and the bathroom floor too and all over my sheets too. It's everywhere. And you know what?"

I don't know what. I don't want to know what and I don't know why I'm still listening. But I am.

"It was a moment of beauty," he says. "Of beauty. Because that's when it hits me." He taps his forehead with his thin finger. "That's when I know. I know why I'm here—why we're all here. I know what this world is for."

He stops for a second and takes a sip of his coffee. He sure can hold an audience, that smart old guy. "The world is here for one thing. Just one."

He's got my full attention now.

"This world is here to knock the bones out of us—every one of us—piece by piece and splinter by splinter and agony by agony, until we are just a lump of heaving, shivering jelly. And that's it. That's the whole thing. And the world—the *world* I say—the world will go on knocking it out of us until we get it. Yes it will. And if we don't get it now, we will get it later. In diamonds. Uh-huh."

He sips his coffee like he's finished talking to me, but I know he hasn't, and I'm right. He sets the cup down in a pool of black coffee on the saucer.

"Now this can happen bit by bit in whaddyamacallit—increments—and the bones, they are knocked out of you one by one by one, and you get used to it as you go. You stumble along on some cracked bones and some half-bones and some nubs of bone. And you do what you can. You get by. And sometimes—get this now—you can even end up smiling out of the mass of shivering jelly, which is what you are now, which is what you have become." He is staring at the wall and smiling.

"Some people get it early. The bones are knocked right out of them young, and you look at them—yes, you do—and you see it right away. They are made of jelly. They are substantially jelly and nothing else. And when they smile, they have that jelly look to them. They are up to the eyes in jelly. And they are sometimes kind and good people because jelly has made them that way. Or else they are just a sad heap of defeat, one or the other or both." He turns the coffee cup around in its saucer.

"But those people who don't get it early, get it later and sometimes all at once—and if that happens—if the bones are knocked out of them all at once, then the shock of it is enough to kill them. And often it does just that. It kills them. Especially if they are at the end of their lives anyway. That's what they die of. And you look at those people—yes, you do—and you can see that right away. Those people are about to die of it."

He seems a little deflated, a little drained. Slumps over his coffee. "I'm halfway there myself," he says.

And then he looks at me sideways, like he's about to ask me a question such as "What city do you hail from?" or: "How's that homemade pie?" like he's in the year 1935 or any other damn year before I was born. And like I'm right there with him.

TATS AND TORMENTS

Edward is sitting on top of his red VW van. It's rusted round the wheels, round the doors, under the front fender and round the back by the exhaust. It's a beat-up old pile of shit. Trash heap of the 70s, should've died long ago. He knows it. Won't let it go. It still moves, that's the thing. It still rolls right on when it wants to. The gears choke, the choke slips, it groans and complains, but it can still take him places, places he wants to go. Just—not now. Right now, it's tanked and isn't going anywhere.

He's pulled over on the shoulder of the highway, sitting cross-legged on the roof, sipping the dregs of an instant coffee from a paper cup. His last coffee grains are in that cup. Lumps of congealed powdered milk float about. No sugar. None left. It's 5:00 in the morning. He looks round. Dry scrub to his right, beyond that sand and the black smudge of mountains, to his left the empty highway. He is on his way. Knows the thing he is after. Has the plan all worked up and ready to act on.

The rising sun spews up a real display—a fine showing of

rubies and tangerines. Tall cactus plants shadow down in the blood light. Stand like soldiers at attention, watching him. Jesus. They are not. They are just plants, right? And they are not watching him. Could be, though. They look like people standing there, idiot still, looking at him.

What now? Consider the plan. Step through it, front and side. Then, take action.

Step one: Fix the van. Get to Palm Springs. Technically two steps, but call it one. Two halves of one.

Step two: With the stash he's saved up from drywalling and living out of the van for six years, rent a small shop front. Small but tasteful and well accoutred.

Step three: Hire some desperate runt to help with the painting and the window display.

Step four: Get this guy to paint in large white letters on the window: Tats and Torments. At which point the guy will probably ask: "I don't want to be nosy, but why 'torments'?"

"Because it sounds like a good name."

"Yeah, but what is a *torment* in this case? I mean, why on a tattoo shop?"

"A torment is a particular kind of tattoo, one I specialize in and one I am a master of, as it happens."

This is not true, but it shuts the guy up.

Step five: Open shop.

Ok, there might not be a *lot* of people in Palm Springs who want tattoos, but there will be some. And those some—they will be as rich as angels or gods, and he will charge a fucking fortune for a butterfly on a fat arm, an emperor's ransom for a snake on a floppy butt. The riches are there in Palm

Springs plus the scenery is nothing to cough at. The scenery is a rare thing.

Now the sun cringes yellow and the sky is showing its own depressed face. Sand sloughs along under a morning breeze. Some kind of mole or mouse skitters under the van by the back wheel. He remembers hearing that Elvis Presley ate squirrels as a kid, but he doubts that. A squirrel would taste like a mouse and there wouldn't be much meat on it.

Edward drains his cup, slides down off the back of the van, opens the side door and climbs in. It's an interior of a van gone rogue, gone AWOL, gone to the ninth degree of entropy. It's a dark, dank chaos in there. Debris of his life everywhere. Dirty socks, chicken bones, boxes, broken plates, the stink of a sleeping bag he sleeps in, and the rust doing its work even in here. No seats, he tore those out years ago, only the driver's seat left. The floor has a hole in it rusting out from the centre.

Edward crawls round that hole to the back, picks up a cable and uncircles it. This is a specialized cable—NCA 230 Volt, made just for the tattoo gun he bought last week. Paid an aristocracy for that gun. But it's a Firehawk 390, extreme rotary, dwarf handle, and eighteen vari-sized needles to go along with it. The. Very. Best. Anywhere.

He crouches down. Opens up the white shiny box, takes the tattoo gun out. It's a sleek mink, a lady's dancing shoe, a stiletto blade, fine and bright polished. And it's his.

He runs his finger along its neck, taps his thumb on the handle. He is just going to try this sucker out—just once—before he fixes the van, gets it started and rolls on to Palm

Springs. Just once. For the joy and the purity of it, the sweet anticipation. Just this once. When this beauty gets to work, it will be the dream and the serenity that will claim his life.

He attaches the cord to the handle of the gun, plugs the other end into his battery in the van. Switches it on. Nothing. What the fuck? He scratches his beard, the grey of it scrabbles across his chest. He crawls back out of the van. Walks around the van a couple of times, his breaths coming hard and rattling fast. Calm down, right? Think this out. Think this through. Front and side. It must be the cable. Or the connection in the gun. Or what? *What*? He can't test the cable on anything else, it is specialized to the tattoo gun. He knows the battery is ok because his electric toothbrush is plugged into it and the base light is on, winking blue.

He remembers brushing his teeth at 3:00 this morning in preparation for the last leg of his trip to Palm Springs. There is no better feeling than fresh teeth, an empty highway ahead, and the certain knowledge that Palm Springs will soon be in sight. He tries to hold on to that memory, calm his mind, calm, right? But all he can think of now is: the battery is working, so it must be the tattoo gun. It's stubborn, it's playing dead, it's out of its mind, or it's fucked.

He climbs back into the van to deal with the problem. Because deal with it he must. It's what his plan hangs on. So, yes.

He crawls to the back and picks up the thing like it is made of dragonfly wings, gentle as an angel, detaches the cord, and like he is an ER surgeon with the patience of a fallen saint, re-attaches it, gentle, gentle, closes his eyes, prays, and pushes the start button. Nothing.

He grips the tattoo gun, sleek as a mink, shiny as a lady's dancing shoe, a precision, fine-tuned instrument of the highest quality and price, and smashes it against the inside wall of the van. It takes him a long time and many hits to break it. It is so well made it resists all his efforts, won't pander to destruction. But eventually, it gives up and cracks a death grin down one side. Edward tosses the broken machine into the hole in the floor. He rummages under some KFC boxes and pulls out a hammer.

With the hammer he smashes all eighteen vari-sized precision needles. He pounds each one until it breaks. Sometimes they jump away from him in fear or consternation, but he finds them and puts them back on the floor in front of him and pounds away until they are shattered into a shock pile of metal shards and scraps.

He puts the hammer back under the KFC boxes and crawls out of the van. Begins to walk down the shoulder of the highway. He walks a long way. A few cars pass him. The sun is a fiery, hot-tempered sun, screaming its disgust at him. Needling him with burning insults and accusations.

The sun glints off a tiny metal cylinder lying by the side of the road. Edward picks it up, turns it over in his hand and takes the plastic lid off. Inside, a roll of film. He unscrolls the film and holds it up to see what the pictures are. That would be something. To see some pictures here. Maybe a picture of Palm Springs. Of a lady dancing in Palm Springs. No pictures. Just one damn empty frame after the other. He tries to tear the film up, but it won't tear. It resists destruction. All his efforts. What it is made of, it is a plastic mixed up with tungsten and graphene. He tears, he screams, he bites at it, pulls it this way and that, bends over, boots down one end, tries to rip into it from the side, from the end. It won't tear. He tosses the empty cylinder into the scrub, the film onto the highway.

And walks on. Under the punishment of the sun.

PEST

She is a parasite with grey hair and a slight moustache. Every time I use the photocopier, she stands right beside it and asks me what I'm doing. Or she tells me about the last document she had to copy, if a page was lost or torn, or if there was a paper jam and how she had to fix it. Sometimes she tells me about her personal problems, her eyebrows hunching in together to console each other like sad caterpillars. As I try to copy my document, she shrieks at me about her sick cat that vomits on her carpet.

And the worst is she stands so close to me — less than a foot away — while I'm trapped at the machine, and I can even feel in the pit of my own stomach the lacerating insistence of her anxiety. Her voice is grating — harsh and pitched up like a sick angry crow, sometimes swooping down into that miserable Kardashianism called "vocal fry".

She's always watching, waiting for me to head for the photocopier. In our open-plan office, I can see her as she gets up from her desk to meet me there, always wearing the same crumpled-up blue skirt with a stain on it and whitish blouse with yellowed shoulders. She must know she annoys me, must know I am far from the willing listener she's looking for. I respond only in grunts to whatever she says. Most times I don't even hear what she's saying. I force myself to think as loudly as I can about dinner, the benefits of tempeh over tofu, anything — just to shut out that horrible bird screech in my ear.

I never look her in the eye. I don't want to see the lines of self-pity etched into her face just around the edges of her moustache. And I don't want to see her permanent sad emoji mouth. I can't look at her. It makes me wild to look at her. She must suspect this — at least she must wonder why I never look at her — what does she think, I'm her BFF or what? Why does she persist in tormenting me?

No one in the office speaks to her. No one. I think she's been through all eight of us, loaded each one of us with her problems, her shrieking presence — and she smells. There's a permanent body odour of unwashed clothes and ancient sweat, and her breath stinks like she's been recently exhumed against her will. Lately, that smell has leeched on to me.

But even with all this I still can't figure out why I hate her so much. Why she annoys me beyond my limits, why I often feel I could just staple up her mouth with the staple gun, photocopy her face with the lid down, smack her upside the head with the hole punch. I don't understand it — she just — has this effect on me — within six feet of her I can feel my jaw locking, my heart trying to leap out of my ribcage, and my blood pressure rising up like a tsunami in a test tube.

It's becoming a health and safety issue. Got to do something. Whenever I see her—I—I fly into a panic.

I've tried talking to my co-workers about her, but they just don't want to listen. Either they walk away from me, or their eyes glaze over, and lately they have begun to look at me strangely. I guess I've been insisting too much. I've been to HR three times, but they say that unless there is evidence of assault or harassment, they can't do anything. Wish we had a union. We don't.

Just two days ago, when I had a deadline to copy six statements of claim and bind them, she sprinted to the copier to meet me, told me her cat vomited three times that morning and she might have to take him to the vet. What could she do if her cat was really sick? She could never have him put down. Never. As the machine was spitting out the pages, I glanced at her. This time she was really upset. Her voice dropped an octave and there were tears in her eyes. Her face was contorted—holding in riptides of emotion that were taking her under. I saw that. Hell. I could feel it. No one will help me, she said, no one will listen. I can't live on my own without my cat—her voice began to rise again, stepping up word by word to sick crow pitch. And what if my cat dies? What should I do?

I looked at her. "Don't worry about it," I said. "Forget it. Everything will be fine." I picked up my copies, but she was standing right in front of me. "Get out of my fucking way!" I yelled. "Can't you see I can't help you?" I went over to the binding machine and left her standing by the copier. I didn't see her again that day.

When I got home, I thought about her, how she annoys me, how rude I am to her. It's not—me. I'm a good-natured, easygoing person—also kind. I can really put myself in another person's shoes and feel what they feel. I have the imagination to do that. If it is empathy you want to call it, then I have it. So—so why am I so rude to her? Why is it I hate her—in 3-D bright red, blood deep? What is it about her that is pushing me over the edge? Because over the edge I will go if I don't do something about it. She is—getting under my skin and crawling around under there.

At the end of the day, I remember everything she's said to me—every single high-pitch word, and I can even see that horrible crumpled blue skirt and that yellowish blouse wishing to be white. I smell that smell of old sweat. Maybe it's an actual chemical or energy field she's sending out—a poison aura. Look. She is just a horrible, miserable, annoying person. That's it and there is nothing I can do about it. Last night I was thinking that since there is nothing I can do about it, I may as well try and be nicer to her. If I can.

So. This morning, I brought her a latte and put it on her desk. But she wasn't in the office all day. That's unusual. Maybe she was looking after her cat. I had a calm peaceful day and got a lot of work done since my stress level was down about ninety points. Just before I left the office, I got a message from HR—they want to see me tomorrow. I don't know what it's about, but maybe they have found a solution?

Right now, I'm sitting on my bed, thinking about what I should do. I'm trying not to panic but I'm about to go over the edge with this person tormenting me all the time. Even when she's not here, she's here. I sense her presence, and sometimes I can even almost see her—like right now, she is sitting beside me, less than a foot away. Needling me, ferreting around under my pillows, looking for something, poking my arm and my head. Now she's telling me to clean the dishes in the sink, she's telling me to clean up the mess on the carpet, she's telling me to take the cat to the vet. She's telling me to wash my clothes. She's harping on and on—she won't shut up. I can't stand her sick crow voice and the smell—it's suffocating. How did she get in here anyway? Can't I ever get away from her? Won't she leave me alone? I've told her I detest her, I've told her to get out, but she won't go. Now she's rummaging through all my things on my dresser, muttering about a comb.

STILLCHILD

He looks asleep. He's not. He surveys the scene to see what might be threading through the gloom—one wending its way, or skipping home after extra-curriculars, alone and waifish, angel-light and golden-haired, toting a little knapsack and traipsing home, all unsuspecting, all innocence and light of heart.

He lies in want, alone. He won't wait long. In his rearview, a tiny figure. No, not viable, this one, crossing over the street now, too late. No, she's heading back this way, zigzagging back to him. She approaches the car.

He rolls down the window, tells her that her mother has asked him to drive her home. She hesitates. He smiles and opens the door, and she gets in. He locks the door.

Night is closing in now and closing in fast as the car speeds out of town and down an empty highway.

In less than an hour, the mother on the rack, the police out in force. By morning, neighbours are out too, stepping with care, side by side through long grasses, backyards, empty lots, schoolyards, and ravines.

When the police find her hours later, she is dazed and walking along the edge of the woods between the highway and the trees. Apparently, the only thing missing — the knapsack.

They drive her home and she runs into the arms of her mother, and her mother holds her for minutes, won't let go, weeping and stroking her hair.

She is alright. She is alright. At home, she drinks apple juice, eats toast and peanut butter, and the next day she plays with her friends in the schoolyard. She is alright. She returns to school when her mother is certain she can manage, and she goes to all her classes and completes all her assignments. She is alright. She laughs with her friends, goes to birthday parties, sleepovers, and bakes cupcakes with her friends in her mother's kitchen. They watch her carefully. She looks the same. Is the same. She is alright.

She is not. Inside, she carries the child she was when she died. The dead child. The murdered child that lay in a ditch, her golden hair transgressed with mud, her face turned sideways to the earth, leaves raked loosely over her body. And as the girl grows, the dead child stays with her, sits on her pillow at night and whispers stories, teaches her the ways of people, scrawls weird words on the walls of her room, guides her, all smiling, through the dark warp of dreams. In the morning, the stillchild holds herself wall-eyed and hollow-hearted before others who would come near, keeping them always at bay with a little clenched fist. And if the woman dares speak, the child turns to her, lays her finger against her lips and calls the woman to silence. And she wraps her earth-stained arms around her, cradling her in shame, holding her. Still.

ICICLES

The bandage ripped. I tore it.

Here is a picture of the cat I had when I was twelve. She bit me once, so I hit her with a stick. Went into the bathroom and cried in the bathtub.

I need a new bandage. And six new teeth.

It's cold out today and rainy too. And this is where I am. Right here in front of you—no use denying it.

Crawled out. Seventy-nine thousand of them. I got approximately eight of them as they left. Had to burrow in to get them though. Nasty but necessary.

And here is a picture of me on a swing, age eight. That's my father standing beside the swing. Smiling and holding the AK-47. Aiming right at me.

You say there is a cut—another one, here? That's not a cut. That's a viable escape route.

I'll go get some CoverGirl tomorrow when some money

comes in. It acts like plaster on my face so the cuts don't show.

Seventy-five of you is not enough to understand. Or even to begin to try to. So don't.

Check this: I went to a really good school. I wore a uniform. It was green with a yellow shirt.
I sang hymns: "All things bright and beautiful. All creatures great and small."
I had all my teeth then. Here is a picture of that school. Red brick walls and tall narrow windows in the walls and about 150 million of them crawling through. Right now.
I was twelve when I got thrown out of that school.

You think I don't know what I should do? I've spoken with sixty-eight of them—social workers, doctors and psychiatrists, do-gooders and helpists (those are the ones on a real fucking mission). I know what I should do.

It'll take about 150,000 of you to even begin to understand what this is like. And even then, you won't. You never will. Because you are not in the Monoverse.

I had breakfast today. Track my arm. You can see the leftovers. Listen. Check this: I lived in a real house once. It had bricks and a roof. And windows. And a mother in it.

Here is a picture of that house. See the plastic wading pool in the backyard, under the apple tree? I used to pretend to swim laps in that thing. The neighbour drowned in it. Or that was me. My mother was inside, watching through the kitchen window, drinking a martini and waving and laughing.

That's a battalion of them just under my skin now, on my left arm, causing those cuts. I don't do it. They do. And I need a knife sometimes to get them out. I've had four skin grafts. Four. Ripped all of them off. Sometimes I do that. Not always. Only when they get in the way.

Monolith. You try and tear it down. You can't, Little Monkey.

That's what my father used to call me: Little Monkey. He didn't know my real name.

Check this: Here is a picture of my mother. That's her throwing the grenade. That one in that picture landed in the backyard and blew up the apple tree when the cat was in it. That was intentional. I picked fur out of the grass for months. Spite is a terrible thing.

That grey car is the new grey cop car vehicle disguised as a grey family car vehicle. It comes round here every day and the cops in it think I don't know.

Princely deceptions.

What they don't know is: I see through the glazed windows of that car and I know how many of them there are in there, waiting for me to come out: Nine.

About fifty crawling through right now. Good thing I still have fingernails.
Fingernails are not like teeth. They are made of a different substance.
They don't rot with abuse; they just keep growing. Even in

the grave they will grow.

A shopping cart is unfortunately not opaque. Or waterproof. But put a few garbage bags on it and it will hide you from the Deception Vehicles cruising by.

Listen. I've been here years, so don't fret about it. I'm a tough nut. My mother said I was and she would know. She said I was strong as an ox. I am, too. She got that right.

I can survive anything.

Tomorrow I'm going to check in. Just watch me. In a couple of months, I'll be doing secretarial work in a government agency. With dentures. You won't recognize me.

I can change all this. I can.

I hear the president fell over. I read the news. I keep up with it. Everything. Current events. Entertainment news. Cultural phenomena. Who's trending. Who isn't. Like you. You're trending. I know who you are.

Cover that hole in your stomach. It's radioactive. I can see gamma rays of hurt streaming out from the pit. That's not good for your health.

Here is a picture of me holding the cat. I'm smiling in this one. That's unique.

Now. I'll get a knife because there are forty-three of them crawling through my wrist at this moment. I can feel them. Hatching and crawling. Know what that's like?

Listen. At my eighth birthday party, I had a white cake with pink icing that said "Happy Birthday" in green icing and candles shaped like Mickey Mouse and ballerinas. It was a lot like your birthday cake at the same age.

You're leaving?

Don't go.

If you don't see me tomorrow, it means I'm bleeding out somewhere. Or shopping.

I won't be here but I'll be some place. Catch the light. It's beautiful now the rain has stopped. Icicles falling in blue sky.

Look.

Don't go.

Wait.

Check this: It's a picture of you. Here you are at my birthday party grinning out at the camera. Stinking of joy. I think that's you. You might not think it is, but it is. You've got my eyes. You've got my bones. You've got my blood in your mouth.

THE ONE ABOUT

The rain fell heavy and he never stopped walking. He was drenched and his clothes stuck to him, he was clammy and cold in the wet, but he never stopped walking, he walked faster and faster, his shoes buckets of water, walking walking in buckets of water and the rain fell heavier and heavier until it hurt his head and soaked into his skin and into his sneaking bones and it was pounding down now, driving down torrents on him, now windswept and drilling sideways into his head, the sky black, but he would not stop nor would he take shelter.

He took pleasure in this decision to walk because he had not one dog-mauled scrap of an idea what else he could do. And the rain might help. The rain might force desperation, force him to take action, or make a plan, or get a job, or think of:

No, better call a friend or read a book. Go home and watch a video: Sia, Adele, Rihanna, Amy, Billie. Steal a car and drive to Detroit. Why Detroit? Could be Chicago.

Climb up the stairs of an eighty-storey condo, up up to

the roof. Howl at the black moon and wait for the echo to howl back, rage out blind in the dull dementing night. Then think of:

No. Rob a bank and buy a condo. Memorize words—any words all beginning with *f*. Start with: Future. Futile. Fantastical fury fentanyl fluorescent fabricate funicular. Fool. Tell a joke—the one about—Take a walk down a neuronal pathway, dissolve in the rain. Eat an ice cream cone, curse God—what God—curse Nietzsche. Invent a god, any god. Fake it through just fake. It. Through. Be fly.

Think of a small startup business, a money-making enterprise, yes, that's it. A YouTube channel. Call it Whizzshit and play videos of how-to lectures framed in toilet bowls. A million hits, yes, or a tattoo place, a million holes. Call a friend? Go to the gym. Work out the body til the high-flying mind peaks and with a parabolic glide, folds up, stops. Think of:

No.

Sing Broadway tunes to the davening scholars of Talmudic law, crown the faithful with the stolen halos of angels, bless them in anger, sing "Hallelujah" and capsize the crib-bound baby Jesus. Tap dance on the heads of martyrs. Plead the fifth and go down singing. Get a tattoo. Needling pain punctuating each minute so it feels alive. Feels. Think of:

No. Run to the end of the damn city of the damned just keep going in the rain. Learn a new language learn eight. Italian, French, Farsi, Pashto. Send a text. To the ex? Hi, so great not to hear from you in so long and then a string of: grinning emoji cats yellow faces teared up with joy hahaha. Delete delete. Delete Snapchat. That is a must do.

Buy a wingsuit and skydive off the edge of the Earth. Call a friend. Hope to, hope not to — think of:

No. Tell a joke, the one about — call a crisis line and scream flaming white murder at them, cannibalize their sympathy, mock their warm forgiving hearts — the ground zeros of hypocrisy — until they hang up. Cut off an ear and send it to the ex. With a note that says: I *am* listening. Then go to Emergency. Think of:

No. Tell a joke to the triage nurse, the one about — sit there, bleed, life chuckling and frothing out of the sliced skin, easy as that. Then think of:

No. Take a peek round the curtain. Watch people in their last moments. Count the snake-rattling breaths — there are videos of that. Watch the seep of blood the spill of life all the pain of losing and the loss of love. Arms reaching out for other arms and the tears flowing freely and the wailing of grief. Feel. That. Feel. Think of:

No. Puke in the sink the yellow bile. Drop acid, drop — there are videos of that too. Hallucinate the end. Go lucid. Envision the life hereafter. See the spirit drift up from the body. Wild luminous colours, the soul coughing itself out into white rainbows and the beauty of the last firing swan-singing neurons. Ultimate consciousness. Paradise then. No. Such. Luck. Cut it. Think of:

No. Call a friend. Invent God. Go to a party. Text. Check. Facebook. Check. Reddit. Check. Drink tequila, tell a joke, listen to a joke, think of:

No. Tell another joke, the one about — think of:

No. Run. Run in the rain and keep going just keep going

til lungs burn from the shear and suck of air. Run and let the rain torrent down all over, all over and in and in and brain deep, just keep on running and think of:

No. Remember—what—what? Think of:

No. Not that.

SWING

At the inquest they establish cause of death and you stand there in the courtroom, your eyes watering, your arms twitching, your hands flapping.

You look up at the coroner behind her high desk and say: "Listen to me. I'm breathing. I'm here."

But she looks doubtful. And you sigh and turn to the witness and say: "What did you see?"

And the witness, an old retired lawyer, tells exactly what he saw: how you fell under the knife, how you got carved up and quartered, how he had to turn away from the tragic scene so as not to see the gore.

And you step up to this witness and say: "Sir. You are mistaken. Here I am, ready to do whatever is needed to prove it."

And once, when you were a tiny thing, you learned to tap dance. You had the shoes, the black ribbon, the metal tips — you have them now — and the steps come back to you.

You dance lunatic in the courtroom, swinging those arms, Shirley Templing it in front of this damn old retired lawyer — shuffle toe, shuffle heel, slide tap, slide tap, step, ball change.

"Come on! Look!" you say and muster up a drum roll of taps, tripping the light fantastic.

And he's staring at you like you've lost the thing that makes you human.

And so you reach out and take his hand and say: "Be my witness now."

But he turns away from you. He studies the charts and the X-rays of broken things, smashed things, things torn apart. And he looks convinced by the evidence of the gravity of the situation. He's just waiting for the coroner to pronounce—any second—that's clear enough—unless you can put a stop to this.

So in your tap shoes you Fosse up a whole roaring lost generation of a routine—clickety, clackety, kick, ball change, your arms flying—it's showtime! And you're selling it with a wide-ass grin, you're killing it, hoofing it up in this razzle-dazzle routine, the cakewalk thrill of it, stretching out your arms, and beckoning him to join you.

And yes—now—the old lawyer in his creosote-coloured suit slowsteps down from the witness box and starts to shuffle and thrust his hip replacements from side to side— he's with you!

He's doing the Charleston, segueing into lambada, his arms twitching and swanning—and it's—fantastic—he's wholly involved in this—dancing the life out of it—dancing the life back into it.

And the coroner is watching all of this from up there behind her high desk—and finally, finally—she brings down the hammer hand with a grave thud and yells: "Insufficient evidence! Case dismissed!"

And you laugh you cry you bow to your witness you tap your way down the aisle past the empty seats and waltz out of that old courtroom and push open those coffin lid doors and let them swing and swing and swing behind you.

ACKNOWLEDGEMENTS

My thanks to the following journals where these stories first appeared:

'Forsythia' in *The Quilliad*, 'Worse' in *filling Station*, 'Night Room' in *The Bookends Review*, 'The Sandcastle' in *Just Words Anthology*, 'The Lammergeier' in *Orca, A Literary Journal*, 'Leaving You' in *Into the Void* (2020; nominee for Pushcart Prize and for Best Small Fictions), 'Beyond Poland' in *Bryant Literary Review*, 'Inside the House Inside' in *Variant Literature* (2021; nominee for Best Small Fictions), 'Wall of Glass' in *ANMLY*, 'The Fret' in *Paper Teller Diorama Anthology* (2021; nominee for Pushcart Prize), 'Laugh Riot' in *The Lincoln Review* (2022; nominee for Pushcart Prize), 'Panic Room' in *Fatal Flaw*, 'Yellowcake' in *Litro Magazine*, 'Black Water' in *Thrice Fiction*, 'come back & no don't' in *The Temz Review*, 'Renter' in *filling Station*, 'You   Body' in *The Masters Review* (2023; winner of Second Person Short Story Contest), 'Tats and Torments' in *Stand Quarterly of the Arts*, 'Stillchild' in *Spelk*, 'Icicles' in *Litro Magazine*, 'The One About' in *Anti*lang, 'Swing' in *The Gravity of the Thing* (2021; nominee for Best Small Fictions).

I would like to thank Wendy Atkinson at Ronsdale Press for her invaluable support and suggestions, Robyn So for her careful and detailed edit of the manuscript, Kevin Welsh for the thorough proofreading and David Lester for the book design and powerful cover.

I'm grateful to my family and friends for their support and encouragement in putting this collection together: Jonathan Goldsmith, Penny Goldsmith, Kelly Cade, Aidan Cade Goldsmith, Thula Cade Goldsmith, Jon Campbell, Yashin Blake, Joanna Marcus, Sandy Sanghera and Cynthia Flood.

ABOUT THE AUTHOR

Rosalind Goldsmith's short stories have been published in literary journals in Canada, the U.S. and the U.K. Before writing short fiction, she wrote radio plays for CBC Radio Drama, a play for the Blyth Festival Theatre and translated and adapted short stories by the Uruguayan writer Felisberto Hernández for CBC Radio. She is a volunteer facilitator with the Writers Collective of Canada and tutors literacy for adults. Rosalind lives in Toronto: